BRODERIE ANGLAISE

There was a ring at the door. Alexa went pale. There was the sound of voices: Jeremy's shrill, rather effeminate, with long-drawn-out vowels, then another which beside his seemed deep, almost masculine. A voice that was soft, full of hidden depths, crepuscular.

My God, thought Alexa, I'd forgotten about her voice!

The door opened. A woman appeared. She was of medium height, wearing a tight-fitting, very simple tailored suit that followed the lines of her graceful but plumpish form.

If she wasn't so well proportioned her head would look too big, Alexa noted with a beating heart.

Her features were irregular; her nose turned up, her mouth was too big and her lips were too thick. The upper lip was arched and protruded slightly over the other. The eyes, shaded by a hat with a turned-down brim, were laughing, but small. Where was the siren John had described?

Anne Lindell wasn't even pretty.

VIOLET TREFUSIS

BRODERIE ANGLAISE

Translated from the French by
BARBARA BRAY

A Methuen Paperback

A Methuen Paperback

BRODERIE ANGLAISE

First published in Great Britain 1986
by Methuen London Ltd
This edition published 1987
by Methuen London Ltd
11 New Fetter Lane, London EC4P 4EE

Published by arrangement with
Harcourt Brace Jovanovich, Inc

Printed and bound in Great Britain by
Richard Clay Ltd, Bungay, Suffolk

British Library Cataloguing in Publication Data

Trefusis, Violet
Broderie anglaise.
I. Title II. Broderie anglaise. *English*
843'.912[F] PQ2638.R3

ISBN 0–413–60100–5

INTRODUCTION

Broderie Anglaise was first published in 1935. Like Violet Trefusis's previous two novels, it was written in French and has never, until now, been reprinted or translated into English. Violet spent most of her adult life in France, where she had a house that she loved, in the country near Paris, and countless friends in the worlds of high society and the arts. She was always happier in France than in her native England; in the 1930s, before the Second World War drove her temporarily back over the Channel, she was, as she said in her autobiography *Don't Look Round*, at her zenith.

This novel, written in that confident time, is a considerable literary curiosity, presenting Violet's fictional version of the key event of her youth: her affair with Vita Sackville-West. Violet did not discuss this explosive episode in later life, nor is it referred to in her autobiography, though that book contains a romantic description of Vita and an account of their childhood friendship. Since Vita's death, the story has been fully told—in her son Nigel Nicolson's *Portrait of a Marriage* (which includes Vita's own account), in James Lees-Milne's biography of Harold Nicolson, and in my own biography of Vita—from different perspectives, but all basically focussing on Vita. Violet had collaborated with Vita on *Challenge*, the romantic novel about themselves written while they were still together. In 1928 Virginia Woolf had given an even more imaginative version of their doomed alliance at the beginning of her novel *Orlando*, where Violet appears as the "faithless, mutable, fickle" Russian princess who abandons Orlando on the day they were to elope together. Violet's two biographers, Philippe Jullian and Henrietta Sharp, went over the ground too, with sympathetic understanding for Violet's personality and problems. And meanwhile, in this forgotten and out-of-print French novel, Violet Trefusis had already had her say. That is why *Broderie Anglaise* is worth reissuing, in English, and why it is worth reading. It has been rescued from oblivion by the enthusiasm of her loyal friend and literary executor, John Phillips.

Violet Trefusis chose to make the central character, the only one whose thoughts we share, not herself or Vita but Virginia Woolf—or a highbrow English novelist, Alexa, who is based on Violet's impression of Virginia Woolf. It is not an exact portrait; Alexa has none of Virginia Woolf's acid wit and seems chiefly preoccupied by her rather superficial romantic needs. Violet, who in spite of her intelligence lived on her emotions and her instinctive shrewdness, was unable or unwilling to suggest any real intellectual capacity in Alexa. If, as I believe, her aim was to demythologize both Vita and Virginia, she certainly succeeded with Virginia.

Violet Trefusis knew about Vita's later and very different relationship with Virginia Woolf. She would have known from *Orlando*, even if she had not heard from friends in common, such as Raymond Mortimer; she would have known, from the same sources, that Vita had told Virginia all about *her*. In *Broderie Anglaise*, Violet herself is represented by Anne, who pays a traumatically significant visit to Alexa/Virginia.

Violet actually visited Virginia Woolf at 52 Tavistock Square in early November 1932, in the hope that the Hogarth Press might be interested in her new novel *Tandem*. Afterwards Virginia described the occasion to Vita, who had not seen Violet (now in her late thirties) for years:

> Lord what fun! I can quite see why you were so enamoured—then: she's a little too full, now, overblown rather; but what seduction! What a voice—lisping, faltering, what warmth, suppleness, and in her way—its not mine—I'm a good deal more refined—but that's not altogether an advantage—how lovely, like a squirrel among buck hares—a red squirrel among brown nuts. We glanced and winked through the leaves. . . .

Out of this meeting Violet Trefusis built her novel, and Virginia Woolf's picture of the conjunction between Violet, warm and seductive as a furry animal, and her "refined" self in no way contradicts Violet's own picture of the two in *Broderie Anglaise*. In the novel, Alexa/Virginia thinks of Anne/Violet not as a squirrel but as a fox cub; this was exactly how Virginia had described Violet, as the Russian princess in *Orlando*; and nine years later, in 1941, Virginia indeed wrote to Vita that "I still remember her, like a fox cub, all scent and seduction, coming to 52 [Tavistock Square]."

The structure of *Broderie Anglaise* is very simple. Alexa the spinster novelist, who lives with a literary uncle, is desperately in love with young Lord Shorne (who represents Vita). Alexa is confident as a writer but not as a woman; and John Shorne, though flattered "to be the lover of one of the most distinguished women in England," finds her "an awkward mistress" and refuses to be bound by her. The balance of power is all on his side.

Their relationship is haunted by John Shorne's memory of his first love, his young cousin Anne (Violet). Alexa too is obsessed by the idea of Anne, who seems like "an icon looking down on us day and night." Alexa is perpetually asking John about her and feels she knows Anne "as if she'd created her, every feature, every tone of voice." Just as Virginia Woolf had created an imaginary Violet in *Orlando*, so Alexa has created an imaginary Anne in a novel, to which John has supplied "telling details." John has told Alexa that Anne betrayed him, jilting him on their wedding day. He has never got over it.

Alexa's thoughts flash back to the beginning of her affair with John Shorne, and here we see how unequivocally he is based on Vita. He is handsome in a sombre way, with heavy-lidded eyes and dark hair. Through his mother he has Latin blood; and he lives with her in the great family house, "at once palace and fortress," where the family portraits echo John's own features down the generations. Alexa, who is "the learned daughter of a line of scholars and lawyers," is fascinated by the glamorous history of the Shorne family; like Virginia Woolf, she is a romantic snob.

Violet Trefusis's description of John Shorne's mother is, unambiguously, a portrait of Vita's mother, Lady Sackville. In her autobiography, Violet was later to write of Lady Sackville: "She was a woman of about fifty. In her too fleshy face, classical features sought to escape from the encroaching fat. An admirable mouth, of a pure and cruel design, held good." In *Broderie Anglaise* she had already used almost the same words for Lady Shorne: "a stout lady of about fifty, whose plump face bore the trace of beauty now in decline. Among features fast disappearing amid the engulfing flesh, an admirable mouth stood out, finely etched and cruel."

Lady Shorne/Sackville in her old flannel dressing-gown and curlers, wearing all her jewels at once in a demonstration of power, was something Violet herself must have witnessed at Knole. Vita in *Pepita*, published two years after *Broderie Anglaise*, was to describe her mother going about in a nightgown "of the very thickest and cheapest flannel" as she supervised her household, with "an emerald and diamond brooch of historic value" pinned onto it. Lady Sackville did, like Lady Shorne in the novel, adore the great house and rescue it from neglect; Lord Sackville, like Lord Shorne, was a "mild, contemplative man" who took his only child on "long, silent walks." Other details, notably of John/Vita's early life and dual nature, are equally authentic.

Alexa in *Broderie Anglaise* was seduced by John Shorne

in "the Charles II room," with candlelight glinting on the silver furniture and the tapestries. This is a scene enacted many times before in life and in print. It was in the King's Bedroom at Knole that Vita was first kissed by her future husband; it was there that she had lingered with her early young-girl friends, and it was there that she brought many of her later lovers. It was there, in Vita's novel *The Edwardians*, which Violet would have read, that the young master tries to seduce the doctor's wife. In *Broderie Anglaise* the romantic occasion is ironically diminished: John Shorne is drunk, there are camphor bags all over the bed, and his mother, to Alexa's humiliation, is a party to all that is going on. We get a hint of what is to be the point of *Broderie Anglaise*: John is afraid of his mother, and putty in her hands. Making love to Alexa, he is in some sense making love against, or even to, his dominant mother; there is between mother and son an "intolerable collusion," and "something indecent" about her ascendancy over him.

Everything leads up to, and then down from, the central scene of *Broderie Anglaise*—the unexpected visit that Anne/Violet pays to Alexa/Virginia. Alexa is excited but nervous, and chooses motor cars as a neutral first topic of conversation. She prattles, uncharacteristically, about gearboxes and shock absorbers. Violet Trefusis took this incident not from her own meeting with Virginia Woolf, but her mother's. In her autobiography Violet was to describe how she and Raymond Mortimer had, in her youth, brought Mrs. Keppel to see Virginia Woolf. Anxious to know how the incongruous pair were getting on, they were amazed to hear Mrs. Woolf saying: "My dear Mrs. Keppel, you wouldn't hesitate if you saw the new Lanchester with the fluid flywheel!" Neither lady knew the first thing about motor cars.

Meanwhile Alexa is observing Anne/Violet closely. Alexa's appearance has already been indicated to the reader; looking at herself in the glass before the visit, she noted her thin hair, her scraggy neck, her general air of overrefined bloodlessness. Hair, for Violet Trefusis, was often a symbol of sensuality; in her later novel *Hunt the Slipper* the lovely Caroline's "sherry-coloured" hair is for the first time "freed from restraint" as the hero falls in love with her. In *Broderie Anglaise*, Anne/Violet's hair, in contrast with Alexa's sparse wisps, is "made for struggle—it resists repose." Alexa thinks it looks like "frizzy little red ferns" and acknowledges its sensual significance when Anne removes her hat to reveal "a mass of thick springy hair, curly as vine tendrils."

Violet Trefusis must have had fun depicting herself as Anne. Her worst point was her tendency to put on weight—and it is Anne's. Her best point was her voice; we have already seen how Virginia Woolf reacted to it during the real-life visit. Violet's biographer Philippe Jullian, who knew her, wrote that her voice was "the most fascinating thing about her," and Anne's voice in the novel is described as "soft, full of hidden depths, crepuscular."

Alexa/Virginia, to her amazement, perceives Anne as a happy, warm, natural, womanly woman, an "ordinary" woman, fulfilled in her love of her French home (as Violet was) and in the love of husband and child (as Violet was not). Anne/Violet reproaches Alexa for the way she was portrayed in the latter's novel: "Why make her an intriguer, someone false and treacherous, when really she's only an impulsive little animal?"

Alexa has an even greater surprise coming to her as Anne/Violet reminisces about her long-ago affair with John Shorne—and this, for the author, is the point of the novel. It relates to her own feelings after the ending of her liaison with Vita. She felt, in the sad and lingering aftermath of their alliance, that Vita had let her down. The turning-point for Vita had been when she was given to understand that Violet had let her husband, Denys Trefusis, make love to her: Vita felt, then, that Violet had been hypocritical and let *her* down. Their whole relationship had been punctuated by advances and retreats on both sides. Violet was by no means indifferent to Denys Trefusis; she did not refuse to marry him, and he was, Philippe Jullian states, "a husband whom she valued and to whom she was in some degree attracted."

Both Violet and Vita seem to have gambled recklessly on the strength of their liaison—yet both, all the time, had hedged their bets. Neither was "heroic" and neither was unheroic; the realization of their romantic dream was too difficult. Violet certainly suffered, in the end, more than Vita—who had a close marriage, a home, two children, and an established writing life to go back to. Her luckier circumstances do not however constitute a crime, but a fact of life. Violet was left with a shaky, raw marriage and a vacuum. Her unluckier circumstances do not make her nobler than Vita; she risked damaging fewer people, she had less to lose. These circumstances easily explain why she felt bitter and therefore betrayed. But I believe that Vita, in her stubborn and unflighty way, loved Violet every bit as much as Violet, the "impulsive little animal," loved Vita.

Where Violet in *Broderie Anglaise* falsifies Vita's situation is in attributing John's behaviour with Anne to the unhealthy influence of his mother. But this is fiction—and anyway a legal spouse (such as Vita had) would have made John an adulterer, and his loyalty to that spouse a conventional virtue, and Anne's case would have been considerably weakened. It's true that Vita was in thrall to Lady Sackville, both financially and emotionally. But exactly the same is true of Violet, whose whole life, according to Philippe Jullian, was "dominated by the extraordinary personality of her mother," and who therefore remained "a perennial adolescent." The real "intolerable collusion" that finally separated Violet and Vita was the strange, strong bond between Vita and her husband, Harold Nicolson.

Violet Trefusis was herself a *mythomane*, and she was highly sensitive to the controlling fantasies of other people as well. The effect of Anne's visit on Alexa is to strip away all the mythical glamour that had surrounded both John and Anne in her imagination. Violet Trefusis had the subtlety—and the honesty?—to leave Alexa with a few doubts about the authenticity of Anne's story; perhaps somewhere "between the two contradictory versions" she may be able to save her love for John from disaster. But she knows that he was, indeed, terrified of his mother.

She knows now too that Anne is no *femme fatale* but

a pretty woman with a weight problem, "just like the rest of us. She eats and drinks and laughs and sometimes catches cold." When, after Anne's visit, John returns to see her, he seems different too. Now she looks at him dispassionately; he seems "an artificial character, a summary of all he's read in books and seen on the stage." She finds fault even with his appearance. His dark hair—i.e., his animal attraction—seems less striking. The balance of power between them has shifted. He will love her more now, and she will love him less. The demystification process is complete.

Or not quite. While demythologizing the others, and in some ways herself, Violet builds a whole new fictional character out of Alexa/Virginia's new view of her. Alexa thinks of Anne as the epitome of earthy womanliness, the sort of woman who when everyone is in bed is to be found "soothing the last-born's last sob," and so secure in her femininity that her attraction can only increase with age. This may be self-irony on the author's part, or it may be wish fulfillment; and we should remind ourselves again that this is fiction. In any case there is a pleasing artistic aptness in finding Alexa/Virginia, herself a teller of tales and a dreamer of dreams in fiction, compulsively creating a new myth out of the ruins of the old. There is a concealed pun in the novel's last paragraph: the sweet scent of the flower, or person (*celle* is ambiguous in the French), that must never be mentioned but that Alexa will always carry in secret makes much more sense if its name is—Violet.

Virginia Woolf was not quite so captivated by Violet as Alexa by Anne in the novel, even though she acknowledged her seductiveness to Vita. In her next letter she wrote: "Yes, I see now, in a flash, a chapter in your past I never saw. Frightfully queer. She wasn't what I expected. . . ." To Ethel Smyth, Virginia wrote that she "didn't take to Trefusis, and [she] loves the devil, as I said." After her imaginative flights about Vita and Violet in *Orlando*, meeting the mature Violet, in the flesh, was perhaps anticlimactic—again, a process of demystification. Surprisingly, she wrote nothing at all in her diary about her encounter with Violet.

There were two aspects of the story about which Violet was uncannily right. First, Virginia Woolf *was* troubled by the idea that she was not a "real woman," like Alexa in the novel. But it was in connection with Vita, who had a certain physical opulence, and children, and who could manage a large household, that Virginia felt this. Second, Alexa in the novel ends up seeing John with a less heightened vision and prepares to rebuild the relationship on a lower and more realistic level. Nineteen thirty-five, the year *Broderie Anglaise* was published, was the year in which Virginia wrote in her diary, in March, that "my friendship with Vita is over"; she faced the fact with "no bitterness" but "a certain emptiness." They remained loving friends, in fact, to the end; what was over was the intensity, the fever, and the idealization. To what extent her confrontation with the reality of Violet contributed to Virginia's abandonment of her myth of Vita no one can know. But in any case, as Vita wrote to Violet, Virginia was "a person of strange perception," and so no less was Violet.

Broderie Anglaise was published in Paris, and I do not think that Virginia or Vita ever knew of its existence. There was no copy of it among Vita's books. Even though the surviving correspondence between Vita and Virginia for 1935 is thin, some reference, then or later, to this quite transparent *roman à clef* would surely have got through. Vita and Violet actually met that year, by chance; in October 1935 she and her sister-in-law were in France researching Vita's book on Joan of Arc. Lunching at the Paris Ritz on the way home, they coincided with Violet and saw her again on the channel steamer the next day. "Avoid her," Vita noted in her diary. Little or nothing can have been said.

Violet would have every reason to hope that the people concerned would not read the book. For one thing, Lady Sackville was still alive. Vita would hardly have retained the tenderness for Violet that she manifested in her latter years had she read it. In 1941 she met Violet, a refugee from the war in France, at a country pub for what she called "a queer *à la recherche du temps perdu* luncheon." She told Virginia that Violet had asked "what's known as a leading question about you and me." Virginia was curious to know how Vita had answered; teased and teasing always about Vita's old romances, she asked, "Now why did you love her?"

Neither of them knew that the cunning and fantastical "fox cub" had answered that question herself, in her own way, in print. *Broderie Anglaise* has lain undisturbed for half a century. Now it joins on the shelf those other books that celebrate, satirize, justify, construct, and deconstruct the extraordinary personalities of Vita Sackville-West and of the two women who were most important to her. Vita during the war told Violet that she was an "unexploded bomb"—that is, someone to be treated warily and kept at a distance. In effect, Violet's "unexploded bomb" was *Broderie Anglaise*. It packs no very great charge, but its sophisticated explosion alters the landscape, if only a little.

Victoria Glendinning
London, 1985

BRODERIE ANGLAISE

"Lord Shorne, miss," said the elderly maid, ushering him in.

Alexa remained in the attitude she had just adopted, conveying absorption in her work, obliviousness of the present, and vexation at being thus disturbed.

"Is that you?" she said in a deliberately absent voice, just glancing at him as she finished the sentence she was writing.

But her visitor was not deceived. He knew very well that before his arrival Alexa had consulted the clock a dozen times, wandering back and forth between her desk and the mantelpiece, and that the sentence she was now setting down as if inspired had probably been hanging free for hours.

Selecting a cigarette from his case, he tapped it on the gold cover, lit it with an expert hand and perfect self-assurance, then leaned back in the only comfortable armchair, crossing one leg over the other.

"Had you forgotten me, then?" he said with a quizzical smile. One had to play the game.

"Of course—it was today you were supposed to come! I was so taken up with my work . . ."

The young man gave an ironical laugh.

"Really? Well, if I'm in the way . . ." and he made as if to get up.

Alexa whirled around, shut her notebook, and came and perched on the arm of his chair.

"Aren't I allowed to make a joke any more?" she said with what was meant to be a girlish pout. "He knows very well his Alexa's always pleased to see him, even when he intrudes on her inspiration. Naughty man!" she added, giving a tug at his hair.

"That'll do, Alexa! You know my hair's taboo. Now go and sit on the little sofa like a big girl and listen to what I have to say."

"Oh, I *am* frightened!"—wagging a playful finger.

"Perhaps you're right. Listen and see." He assumed a gruff and facetious tone. "I've just accepted Manning's invitation to spend Easter in Rome."

A heavy silence fell on the pair. Lord Shorne remained quiet, waiting for Alexa to take the lead. The scene would turn out to her advantage or his own according to whether it was treated lightly or seriously. But he was not worried. This was a situation she could not handle. Not feminine enough, he thought pityingly.

"So you're chucking me," she said, with the expected solemnity.

"I don't see that a fortnight's absence calls for so stark an expression. My poor Alexa, why must you take everything so much to heart?"

Her eyes filled with tears.

"Because I love you," she said.

This was just the sort of thing that irritated him most. She was sentimental when she should have been satirical, obstinate when she should have been amenable.

"Loving me doesn't make you very lucid," he said. "I don't intend to spend the rest of my life in Rome. Why do you insist on mixing up the temporary and the terminal, instead of encouraging me to make a trip that will bring me back to you sadder and wiser? If you'd said, 'What a good idea!' " he added with a touch of humour, "I'd have been so surprised I probably shouldn't have gone! Why won't you ever surprise me?"

But his attempt to lead the discussion onto an easier plane was unsuccessful.

"I suppose you're going to Rome," she said, "to see that Pamela?"

"What then?" She had lost the game, and he was vexed at the swiftness of her defeat. "It would be difficult for me not to see that Pamela, as you call her, since as I've just told you she'll be my hostess. My poor Alexa, you jump to such conclusions! How can a woman as competent as you in literary matters be completely helpless—to put it no worse—when it comes to dealing with a situation which anyone with a modicum of savoir-faire would take in their stride?"

"I don't know," she said sorrowfully. "I'm too old to learn."

His attempt to give a light tone to the proceedings broke down before the disarming sincerity of this reply. He felt sorry for her and held out his gold case as if to offer her an arm against himself. But she refused the cigarette of peace, the opportunity of an amicable arrangement. No quarter. She was determined to play the victim. So be it.

"These things aren't learned, my dear," he said. "You're either born a woman, or else—"

"An old maid!" she cried, once more meeting suffering halfway. "Even though I've known what love is," she went on painfully, "I'll always be an old maid. Yes, I shall. It's not a question of virginity—nothing so simple. It's an attitude, a routine that my mind can't throw off. That's why it's so hard for me to keep up with you. You've forced a rhythm on me that isn't my own, a syncopated rhythm I can't get used to."

"We've been rehearsing for five years," he observed drily.

"How you love to humiliate me," she wailed.

"My dear, isn't it rather that you, out of a kind of unconscious masochism, seek the humiliations I try to spare you? Didn't I try to make this a light and friendly conversation? It's you who turned it into a string of bitter and horrible recriminations."

"I'm not taken in by your kindness, John," she replied, stung. "Like all men you have a horror of scenes. If you adopted what you call a friendly tone, it was in the hope I'd sacrifice myself without protest. But I'm determined to do nothing of the sort. If you go, I . . ."

She paused, throwing him a furtive glance to see how far she could go. But his stillness frightened her. Who could say—perhaps he would be only too glad to have done with it all. With a gesture of despair she ran and threw herself at this impassive master's feet.

"Stop torturing me," she begged, clutching at his idly dangling hand and hoping for she knew not what comfort from the contact.

John did not prevent her. It was in his interests to be magnanimous.

"I'm no torturer," he said. "All that's needed is for you to be a bit more sensible, that's all."

The hand condescended to pat her on the head.

"Listen, my little Alexa. Just let me go nicely, without making a scene, and you'll see how affectionate I'll be when I come back. How's that, eh?"

"If I was sure of you . . ." she murmured, grateful in spite of herself at this change of tone.

". . . you wouldn't love me. People only love those they're never sure of."

"Is that why you don't l—"

He put his hand over her mouth.

"Hush! No indecent talk! Anyhow, to come back to Pamela Manning, there's nothing whatsoever to be jealous about. She's a silly little thing, very pretty I grant you, but by the end of a fortnight I'll be fed up with her."

"If only I could believe that," she sighed, clinging to his hand as to a life buoy.

"You can, you can! Come now, Alexa, show a bit of pluck! It's true," he added with genuine interest, "there are two absolutely different and contradictory beings in you, the one who writes and the one who—" he aimed a whiff of smoke at the ceiling—"loves. Why aren't you the woman of your books?"

"I use up all my vital force in my books. There's nothing left over for life," she suggested, with the famous touching smile which was so admired in the literary world but which John found exasperating because it was to be seen in all her photographs.

She was more at ease now that the danger was temporarily averted. Wasn't it always best to expect the worst, so as not to be taken unawares by sorrow? Moreover, any mention of her work had a salutary, therapeutic influence on her. There she was sure of herself, and it was there she could regain lost ground. It was so pleasant to be able to put John right, to browbeat him and show him his own ignorance.

"But," he said—"you won't mind if I say so?—the least of your heroines is so much cleverer than you!"

"They're my own portrait touched up," she answered. "In my books I both ask the questions and give the answers. And also . . . I write with my brain and not with my heart."

"You'll make me believe I was right, and that Alexa the writer avenges herself for Alexa the woman!"

Now that he had got what he wanted he was once more his own charming self, and his fingers stroked the nape of her neck without any guile.

He loved the Alexa of her books. He was proud of her talent and her ever-growing fame. It flattered his vanity to be the lover of one of the most distinguished women in England. Although Alexa was awkward as a mistress and incomplete as a woman, intellectually she was entirely satisfactory. Why, through her inflexibility, must she force him to seek distractions which left him disillusioned and depressed? She knew him so well it was really unforgivable! It would have been so easy for her to stop him from going, just by hiding her dismay. He could feel his resentment returning. Like most complex natures, John was the victim of a very commonplace strategy. He thought he loved a woman, but he really loved a formula, a course of action adapted to all circumstances. Why did Alexa not use the same formula? "I advance, you retreat. You retreat, I advance." It was elementary, as old as the hills. Why did she not set her own personality aside and agree to play a game with all the moves decided in advance? Although he was familiar with this tactic, John would always have let himself be taken in by it.

Meanwhile she was enjoying this all-too-rare truce.

How often would she have to shut her eyes to things in order to keep him? How many more scenes would she have to endure like the one which had just taken place? If only she had been able to consult Anne Lindell and learn to know John through her, as she had learned to know her through him! Anne, this woman who knew everything without having had to learn anything, and who had been as expert at fifteen as Alexa was at thirty. . . .

"What are you thinking about, Alexa?"

The hand became more insidious.

"Nothing in particular . . ."

"You don't want to tell me, but I can guess. What do

we always think about after every scene, every incident? Or, rather, whom?"

In a spasm of rebellion she pushed the demanding hand aside.

"Always the same woman," she exclaimed, "and I've had enough! It's degrading. Really, if we still need her as a witness, we don't deserve to love each other! Haven't we rehearsed long enough to act our parts without having to listen for the prompter?"

"Dear Alexa, it's you who keep thinking about the prompter. You've turned her into a sort of icon looking down on us day and night. With your silent allusions you make me remember someone who ought to have been buried in oblivion years ago. Why try to copy something when we ought to be creating something new?"

"Always her . . . Weren't there other women in your life before you met me?"

"Of course. Passing fancies. She was the only one who mattered."

Alexa gave a groan.

"Here we go again! You're dying to talk about her, to tell me what she looked like, try to describe her voice. Well, I shan't let you. We'll shift for ourselves for once."

She was preparing to fall back on some trumped-up argument or other when she was interrupted by the timely and peremptory ringing of the telephone.

John, left alone, heaved a sigh of relief. The telephone had saved him from another and more dangerous scene, which would have been fatal for him as well as for Alexa.

Would he never manage to banish that ghost? Never have done with the slowly unfurling love which had sapped his youth, taking root in the deepest recesses of his being like a plant that goes on blooming throughout the year without any help from the gardener?

Alexa—what was she but a makeshift? A wearisome substitute, founded on renunciation? "From the ruins of a palace have I built my cottage." What were his caresses but first aid to the injured? He felt a twinge of repulsion.

And yet bonds had come into being between them of a different order—stable, enduring bonds based on a moral partnership, a gradual merging of common interests. Was not Alexa his confidante, the one who had initiated him into those regions of the mind which his own indolent nature made it hard for him to enter? If he managed to get elected to Parliament now, would he not owe his success to Alexa's devotion?

She deserved consideration, and John had made up his mind that the evening they were to spend together should salve all her sorrows. Thank heaven for the telephone!

Ironical and relaxed, he began to stroll about the room he knew so well, with all its frills and flounces. "Really," he used to say sometimes, "your late aunt made marvellous use of her lingerie—this place is the last refuge of the furbelow." The curtains billowed like petticoats. No table was without its lace doily. The cushions were swamped in ribbons. As a setting for Alexa, all this exaggerated femininity looked unhappy and outlandish. But John quite liked the drawing room, finding it stimulating as well as silly, as touching as an old poodle sitting up and begging. He liked it better than Alexa's study, which though tiny was also pretentious, containing, for instance, a forged primitive (bought for a very large sum in Siena), and a genuine Roger Fry which in John's opinion would have been all the better for being a counterfeit.

The drawing room was at least what it seemed.

John was warming his back at the fire when the door opened and Alexa came into the room again. She went and sat in the armchair he had just left. She did not speak, and he looked at her in surprise. Irrepressible excitement was written all over her. Her eyes shone; she was smiling to herself.

"Good news?" he asked nonchalantly, trying to hide his curiosity.

"Excellent."

"So it seems!"

"Oh?"

"A legacy?"

"Why not?"

"Stop trying to keep me guessing, Alexa. Who was it on the telephone?"

"Jeremy Curtiss."

"Oh, him!"

"Yes, but you don't know what he had to tell me!"

John shrugged.

"Some new literary success, no doubt?"

"As it happens, no. It was nothing to do with my literary successes. You think that's all I'm interested in."

"I haven't said so."

"But you think it. Listen, my dear John, I'm going to have to turn you out. I'm expecting a friend to tea."

A look of stupefaction spread over John's face.

"What about our dinner together?"

"You can come back for dinner. No need for you to be here for tea."

"I see—it's a literary affair. Very well. I'll go. I'll be back in time for dinner."

In his relief he gave an affected yawn.

"Don't flirt too much with Jeremy Curtiss."

He kissed her on the forehead and went to the door, annoyed that she did nothing to prevent his going.

Left alone, Alexa threw back her head in a gesture of defiance mingled with exultation. At last she was going to *know*!

A woman at her toilet. A picture by Terborch. No, Vermeer. "Very Vermeer," all these blues. Yes, but in that case she ought to be fair and plump. And anyway, she was not the type to sit looking at herself in the glass. To read a missal, yes, and listen to heavenly voices. Her long fingers were made to tell a rosary rather than wield a powder-puff.

"My hair's thin," she observed sadly, yet with resignation. "My forehead's full and noble, a real philosopher's brow (as we've often said). I've got a youthful eye, an elderly neck, and a finely chiselled mouth and chin. But the whole thing lacks colour. I'm a drawing, a dry-point etching, not a painting."

Ah, well, drawings had their merits.

It was pleasant to think there was not one detail of her person that was not famous, from her nostalgic hats, medieval hands and timid expression to her little handbag that always ended up looking like a half-plucked chicken. The vagueness, or, rather, the limpness, of her clothes lent her movements the undulation of a sea-anemone. She was fluid and elusive; a piece of water-weed, a puff of smoke.

Her face, she discovered, was one of those that are untranslatable to foreigners, arousing in them only pity or scorn. But are not their artificial, simpering women just as ridiculous in the eyes of Anglo-Saxons? No doubt about it! But if the "Continental" females were to be routed they would have to come to Oxford. Meanwhile, was it not best to make good use of the physique which her readers admired, which fitted in with the glory of Oxford, and which had after all made a handsome young man eager to tame her?

She was really being very ungrateful to the body that had so effectively backed up her excellent brain, itself clever enough to shift everything onto an intellectual plane.

"Is my forehead too high? All the better to think with, my dear! Is my body too thin? Other women look vulgar beside me. So much the better if my hair's rather scanty. Too much hair indicates a streak of animality. I should be grateful for my choice and individualistic tresses."

At the end of her inventory she had reached the triumphant certainty that banishes all doubts.

Alexa contemplated her really beautiful hands. Innocent of all polish or other artifice, they were as moving as a couple of shells forgotten by the sea. They seemed to have chosen her as their refuge after having escaped from another body.

Content, she stood up, straightened a lock of hair, then decided that her neck was certainly too thin and could do with some ornament.

The moonstone necklace, or the amber?

The amber. Its tawny fires would lend warmth to her neck.

"How pretty it is! May I touch it? Such a beautiful colour! Like barley sugar!"

"It is, isn't it? A friend brought it back for me from China."

And her eyes would cloud over with memories. She would turn away her head with a sigh. The friend, a sentimental major, died of cholera in Canton in 1925. . . .

Still, the amber was more cheerful than the moonstones—they looked like blind eyes. Unfortunately the amber was really too organic for Alexa's mineral beauty; it brought out her want of sap. She could not aspire to this lushness, this flow: the amber necklace would be like a bowl of resin hung on a dead tree. But Alexa did not see all this. She did not require her jewellery to collaborate with her "type." Such a refinement would never occur to someone so little practised in feminine wiles.

Now she pondered whether she should use the bottle of perfume, still unopened, which one of her nephews had given her for Christmas. Perhaps Jack was too young to make a good choice? He probably did it just to prove to himself how mature he was; when you are sixteen, to give perfume to a woman makes you look like an experienced charmer. Perhaps he had hesitated between the perfume and a pair of silk stockings? She examined the bottle. "Sweet Pea." On the label a girl with upturned eyes clasped to her heart a bunch of enormous flowers. There was a church spire and a thatched cottage in the distance. The girl was undoubtedly devout and right-thinking. Her only vice was the furtive way she crossed sweet peas with gigantic peonies. Horticulture held no mysteries for her. With great care and the points of her nail-scissors, Alexa removed the stopper, then took a deep breath. H'm! It smelt oily and rancid. The perfume had gone off. The girl was only a practical joker. Alexa decided to give the disgraced bottle to her maid—then realised she would be pursued for weeks by the smell of the pseudo-sweet peas. No. The best thing was to get rid of it altogether.

After the problem of the perfume came the problem of the scarf. Alexa's portrait was always taken with a scarf. She was inconceivable without a silk or chiffon scarf. It served as a cloud to soften her over-precise features. She was linked to the rest of mankind by this scarf; it was Fortune's forelock. It was also her weakness, her identification. When anyone wanted to ask her for something, they would give a shy tweak at her scarf. And now, incredible as this might seem, for the first time in ten years Alexa rejected the idea of the scarf. So what, you will say, was she going to do about her neck? As a result of all her attempts at concealment, people probably thought it even thinner and scraggier than it really was. But one had to have the courage to risk one's neck. And after all the amber necklace would help. So Alexa, in a great burst of independence, rejected the scarf, trampled it underfoot. It was all over between them. You can end up being too like your own portrait.

As she was—tall, narrow, contemplative—she would have pleased a fifteenth-century Flemish master, who would certainly have portrayed her with a caged goldfinch and a carnation besprinkled with dew.

On every piece of furniture, bowls, pots and jugs each dutifully produced one or more sickly plants, emerging from their bulbs like little muffled-up invalids. Two or three triumphantly blooming hyacinths seemed to be setting the others an example. It was not so much a bedroom as a hospital for plants. Alexa, the head nurse, made the rounds, rebuking one and encouraging another. In most bedrooms, pride of place is given to the bed, but in Alexa's it was so small and shy you positively had to look for it. It seemed to be apologising for itself. All those laboured flowers, that monkish bed, that parsimonious light, appeared to be waiting for something. What? A vision, an angel visit? Once Alexa, short of space elsewhere, had said her bedroom still had plenty of room.

"Yes, for stigmata!" John said, used to the enormous rooms in his family castle.

Even large numbers of photographs, souvenirs of travel, could not do away with the impression that some visitation was imminent. People and places, rivers and mountains, mingled in wild promiscuity. A Van Eyck Madonna rubbed shoulders with Goya's *Maja Desnuda*. The Dolomites were resigned to being an extension of the Scottish highlands. The blue Danube gaily flowed into the Guadalquivir. These photographs played an important part in Alexa's life. They gave her the right to repose, a state to which she now aspired more than ever. They were witnesses of past motion, and showed, like a veteran's medals, that she too had seen war service—in her case against customs officers, hotel keepers and mosquitoes. Thanks to the photographs Alexa passed for a cosmopolitan in the small enlightened world of Oxford. People would say, "That happened the year you went to Spain," or "This book was published just before you came back from the Dolomites."

As well as the so-called art photographs there were other, more personal ones. John, nonchalant and distinguished, was to be seen in various attitudes. Standing in Copenhagen, sitting in Bordeaux, lying down in Capri.

A sombre beauty was born in his eye, strayed to his too full lips, and reappeared in his classical cleft chin. There was a sort of languid grace about him, a latent fire, which turned this picture of idleness into a figure of rhetoric. His Latin descent—his mother was Italian—showed more clearly in photographs than in real life, where the setting and circle to which he belonged prevented him from looking foreign, making any suggestion of it improbable and even shocking. John himself, with unconscious mimicry, tried to look even taller and more languid still. But the South claimed its own: away from his usual possessive surroundings, he became his true self and wore a beatific smile.

Other frames contained the hygienic countenances of

Anglo-Saxon relatives, whose presence did something to redress the balance disturbed by the languorous images of the young lord.

Alexa was still sitting at her dressing table, on which lay a toilet set of yellowed ivory dating from her twenty-first year. Brushes of all sizes seemed to ask for exercise which Alexa's modest supply of hair could not provide. They had acquired the sulky expression of objects kept for ornament rather than use.

A small green lacquer clock—a gift from three young lady admirers—struck four.

Alexa started, patted her hair again, threw a last glance at her tall, chilly reflection and went to the door. Hardly had she opened it when she was hailed by a man's voice coming from the bottom of the stairs.

"Alexa? Are you coming? Alexa?"

She went slowly down the small staircase. On the last stair, waiting for her, was a big burly man whose blunt features were completed by an enormous pipe. It was always between his lips, and looked like a final piece of carelessness on the part of his Creator. His little mocking eye took in all that was unusual in Alexa's appearance.

"How smart we are today! Who's the fortunate guest . . . ?"

"Wouldn't you like to know!" She wagged an insinuating finger.

"A gentleman of discernment, to judge by the two patches of rouge that adorn your cheeks."

"A lady, Uncle Jim. Unlikely as it may seem, I've gone to all this trouble for a woman."

Her uncle gave her a puzzled look, then burst out laughing.

"Don't tell me! Admit it's just your young lord you're expecting."

"It's someone who is . . . who has been connected with my young lord. But it's not he."

"I see!" the other laughed. "Some rival who has to be routed."

"An ex-rival, rather."

"Well, Alexa"—blandly taking her arm—"don't tell me you're a woman after all!"

"What do you mean by that ambiguous remark?"

"Nothing! But in you the mind towers so high above all the rest I sometimes wonder if you really are a woman. Although . . ."

"Although what?"

"You're determined to make me speak. But I shan't. For five years I've observed the utmost discretion. You don't imagine I'm going to start interfering now in what's none of my business."

"I know. You're the most Olympian of men, and far be it from me to want you to change. But just don't forget I may be more . . . human than you think. That's all. How do you like my hair?"

"It's sibylline."

"And my dress?"

"*Et in arcadia ego*. The frustrated nymph."

"Silly old uncle! Come and see the feast I've prepared."

She led him into the drawing room, where, on a rickety table, lay heaps of buns, muffins, pastries and éclairs (adapted from the French). Uncle Jim was suspicious about the last.

"Éclairs? Is your guest a foreigner, then?"

"Yes. Or almost."

"So the éclairs are for local colour?"

"Yes."

"I was wondering how to describe their colour. I ought to have guessed."

"You're impossible!"

"And where do I come in in all this?"

"You go out! You'd only be in the way."

"Don't I get any tea, then? Not even a crust in the kitchen? You're making a mistake—I could have pretended to be a suitor. A suitor surrounded by éclairs always produces a good effect."

"You a suitor? Have you looked at yourself in the glass? Your presence would only confirm the respectability I've taken a couple of hours to conceal."

"Your visitor's beginning to bore me. What am I supposed to do while she's here?"

"Work. Haven't you got any?"

"No, I haven't! I finished my book on philosophy this morning, and am all ready for some social life."

"Go and see your friend Simpson. You know you usually go and see your friend Simpson when I have friends to tea."

"I have no friend Simpson. He's a myth, a manner of speaking, an alibi."

"I don't want to know. Let him remain what he's always

been: an excuse to run away from this drawing room, which makes your flesh creep."

"Not any more."

"All this just because someone's dropping in for some éclairs!"

"No smoke without fire, no éclairs without thunderbolts.* Éclairs are well-known aphrodisiacs. The ancients—"

"No more of your nonsense, Uncle Jim! Your jokes are becoming lewd. I've always said you should have lived in Elizabethan times, when bawdiness was acceptable. For reasons I cannot go into, I have to see this woman alone. It's the culmination of five years of speculation, introspection and analysis. It's true she'll have someone with her—but I'll see to that. Now go, please, Uncle. By the way, John's coming to dinner."

"Isn't there a Society for the Protection of Ill-Used Uncles? If not, I'll start one. What's more, I'm going straight away to put an advertisement in the paper for a Simpson—a real one this time. You won't be seeing me again this evening. I intend to drain the cup of debauchery to the dregs."

"You just go off nicely now, and we'll expect you at dinner."

"Out of the question! One has one's pride. I wouldn't dine with you if you went on your bended knees. No, joking apart, I shan't be back for dinner. I know an imitation

---

* Translator's note: éclair in French means a flash of lightning; a *coup de foudre*, or thunderbolt, can also be love at first sight.

Simpson who'll be delighted— What am I saying? Overjoyed to have me. Good-bye, you heartless female!"

He was already in the hall when Alexa changed her mind. Wasn't it perhaps a mistake to get rid of him, a devoted friend whose jovial presence might be a great asset? Without him they'd be two against one. And he could take Curtiss off her hands later on, on the pretext of showing him his books.

Alexa hurried into the hall, where Jim was already putting on his rain-coat.

"I've changed my mind. Stay—it will help me if you do!"

"Well! I see your sex has nothing to teach you about caprice. But now my mind's made up, you can exercise your feminine wiles on me as much as you like—"

"Listen, Uncle dear, I don't often ask you for anything. Now I'm asking you to stay. Won't you?"

"Very well. I'll come to your tea party, since you insist, and I'll wreak havoc. But meanwhile allow me to get a little fresh air. The voluptuous atmosphere of the drawing room is too much for me. I'll see you soon."

He threw her a kiss, and the door banged behind him.

Alexa went and sat by the window, at the mercy of the light, now no one else was there. A sluggish drizzle was falling. She looked up at the sky. Its full, baroque clouds were like a gathering of Marlborough's contemporaries—all scrolls and whorls, from their wigs to their shoes. The sky's not very imaginative, she thought, it always reminds me of something.

The drawing room was full of the aroma of tea and

bread and butter, together with the shy scent of daffodils. Alexa put some coal on the fire and resumed her inspection of the tea table. A stranger coming in unexpectedly would have thought it a repast intended for children. It was incredible that adults should ruin their digestion by consuming so many sweet things. Petits fours of an improbable pink flanked pyramids of cream puffs. A chocolate cake oozed with jam. The crevices in the rock cakes gleamed with nuggets of sugar. Not to mention the pots of preserves, or the streak of honey which had burst out of its wooden corset to form a pool of gold.

In the midst of this brilliant company the éclairs, swarthy and glum, huddled together like a surly family which had not been introduced.

Would the visitor appreciate all this, or, as a woman of fashion concerned with personal aesthetics, would she take no more than a slice of bread and butter?

Alexa recalled with satisfaction something the forsaken John had once said: "She's ravishingly pretty, but she has to be careful about her weight." Five years was a long time. Long enough for her to have grown fat. Alexa hoped with all her heart she would be plump, peroxided, and outrageously painted. You do not live in a country like France for nothing.

A little while ago, when Jeremy Curtiss, poor innocent, asked if he could bring with him a "colleague" who was passing through Oxford ("Anne Lindell—perhaps I've mentioned her? She's written two very good books"), Alexa's heart had stopped.

"Anne who?" she had gasped, unwilling to believe her own ears.

"Anne Lindell. She's writing a book about Oxford, and of course getting to know Oxford means getting to know Alexa Harrowby Quince. Please let me bring her—she's leaving the day after tomorrow, and she's dying to make your acquaintance."

On reflection, it was perfectly plausible for a newcomer to literature to want to meet one of its luminaries; natural she should know Jeremy Curtiss (much in evidence in the Paris salons); logical she should be attracted by the intellectual prestige of Oxford. *But did she know?* That was the point.

Alexa spent a long time weighing the pros and cons. Her liaison with Shorne was known only to John's mother and her own servants. Oxford's small literary set regarded Shorne as a young postulant at the Vestal's shrine. It would never have occurred to anyone that the Vestal might have abandoned her principles; even if people had met them abroad they'd have hesitated to describe them as lovers. Alexa's personality disarmed suspicion, and Shorne's age and position in society made such a connection extremely improbable.

No, she was sure Anne's wish to meet her was purely fortuitous, arising out of the combination of circumstances just enumerated.

So, from a comfortable anonymity, she would focus on Anne the spotlight of her own lucidity. Anne? She already knew her as if she had created her—every feature, every tone of voice. "What was she like?" she used to keep asking John. He was quite ready to tell her. And during the first few weeks, when she was still hesitating as to whether to get involved with John, Anne, the false and flighty Anne, had been their main subject of conversation. They kept returning to it as to a drug; it brought them together. . . .

"But just before—didn't she give any sign of what she meant to do? Didn't you suspect anything?"

"Not a thing. She'd never been so affectionate, so ardent."

"Incredible. And you were going to be married the next day?"

"She'd sent for her birth certificate. Her cousin was to act as witness. Everything was signed and settled."

"So how do you explain her leaving you in the lurch like that?"

"I suppose she was afraid of linking her life indissolubly to mine. She had a horror of anything irrevocable. Whenever a decision had to be made, however trifling, it made her quite ill. It was the same with travelling. The only solution would have been to buy tickets to five or six different places, and then have her pick one out of a hat. And she'd still have managed to pick two at once. She was always attracted by the opposite of whatever she did. She'd go from the sublime to the ridiculous.

"Silly things were the only ones she took seriously. She was so contrary that she was only partly satisfied whatever happened. When she ran away from me she was probably obeying some impulse of her own unruly nature. Now

I come to think of it, her faults were those of a restive young animal rather than of a human being."

"You say that to excuse her," said Alexa, jealous.

"Why should I try to excuse her after all the harm she did me?"

"Because you still love her!"

"You shouldn't say that. I'll end up believing it."

"If not, why this morbid need to talk about her, to turn the knife in the wound? It's as if you got a kind of pleasure out of conjuring her up. You turn the French proverb upside down: with you the absent are always in the right."

"Is that the title of your next novel?" he asked, resorting to a characteristic sally.

And Alexa, instead of continuing the argument, retorted: "Why not?"

She got her revenge by talking about Anne's mysterious husband, with whom she was so happy that she had broken with her country and her friends.

Alexa had a power of recovery which sometimes disconcerted John, a way of parrying his blows which he could not help but admire. Instead of the disarray he expected, he would find himself suddenly confronted with a creature of steel, a kind of reporter of the emotions with pen poised to note down anything useful. He liked everything in her that made her different from the other. And it was this Alexa, devoid of all femininity, that attracted him: her accurate and incisive mind, her sound learning, even the virginal air which, by creating difficulties it was gratifying to surmount, constituted her particular charm.

All went well until the day she became his mistress. From then on she knew she was lost. A civil war broke out between her mind and her senses, cutting off all retreat, replacing her multitudinous activities with one lofty preference for the void.

Her passion was like a prince's palace in which she would never be completely at home. She dared not open all the doors—she who had always been content with two or three little book-filled rooms, and who had never known this kind of magic except by hearsay.

She had described it all the better in her books (people like Charlotte Brontë can manage without experience), and now she was sometimes afraid truth might hamper her imagination, which used to get on so well on its own. She felt disorientated, and how could it have been otherwise, with her the learned daughter of a line of scholars and lawyers?

"I don't like to think," John would say, "that there isn't a single prostitute or royal bastard among your ancestors!"

It was amusing to overcome the modesty handed down to her by four generations of scholars.

"You have a perfectly astronomical idea of love," he would say, confronted by her girlish bashfulness.

She could not get used to the idea that John loved her, that John, this privileged being, this Rosenkavalier, was here, hers—that she had the right to touch and caress him. How could she fail to remember the label on every piece of furniture in the castle that was John's country seat, open to the public twice a week and with an atmosphere full of ancient poisons which she breathed in with delight?

How could she fail to remember the young master vaulting over the ropes that cordoned off the furniture, and fleeing the horde of tourists?

And he was here on her pillow—she had only to stretch out her hand to stroke his cheek. "Please do not touch." She did touch him, to get her revenge on the label; but without waking him.

She studied, first with affection and then with apprehension, the face that recalled so many others seen in frames and surrounded by a ruff, a jabot or a stock, a face that had been a type since 1500. Youth could not alter its everlasting structure. Twenty years hence, thirty, it would still appear in all its latent pride, a hereditary face which had come, eternally bored, through five centuries.

How many women had been broken against that cliff? In the case of Anne, was it the cliff itself that had been broken? "Yes, but that was because it wanted to be broken," Alexa couldn't help observing, all too lucid that day. Undoubtedly the cliff had wanted to be broken. And now? Now that it was whole again, would it not summon up the wave to hurl defiance at it? "Higher! Higher still! Lash me, break me if you don't want me to be bored!"

Alas, Alexa could not take it on. Her thirty-seven years were powerless against John's twenty-nine. Since when did the pupil instruct the teacher? She had tried before, without success. It was no easy matter to move John, to scratch the smooth serenity which recognised only one claw and only one way of scratching. Unfortunately Alexa knew nothing of coquetry, of how a woman who is desired can find a thousand and one ways of tantalising with her charms. These are things a man cannot teach a woman; she would need to have watched what other women did. But there was the rub—Alexa had no model: there was nothing to be learned from the wives of Oxford professors. She had only seen the proceedings of ladies; what she needed was a womanly woman, one of those creatures who make men their playthings and can exact a price for their slightest smile. In a word, a woman like Anne.

Meanwhile she had written a book about Anne as conceived of by a woman like Alexa herself: a brilliant, volatile, artificial creature, predictably unpredictable, a historical character, a du Barry who behaved like Lola Montez. In short, a king's mistress.

The general public, with its taste for the romantic, loved the book. It also won enthusiastic praise from the critics, astonished to see Alexa depart from her usual austerity.

Up to a point, John had collaborated with her in the writing of the novel, supplying her with telling details about "the other woman."

The only thing was that, looking back after three years, one's impressions became blurred and distorted. You add a flower here, a piece of lace there. . . . Why? To add interest or colour. . . . And so the woman who was perhaps only a gouache, or a series of vague snapshots, was turned by them, by their combined efforts, into a family portrait worthy to hang in the Long Gallery beside Lely's *Nell Gwynne* and Kneller's *Louise de Kerouaille*.

All the Shornes had had some such episode in their

youth. But John's liaison with Alexa was much less orthodox. It would be difficult to find a place for Alexa Harrowby Quince in the circle of family portraits, unless she was turned into an allegorical figure. Egeria, perhaps, or one of the Muses . . .

"A three-quarter-length portrait of Lord Shorne at his desk, stroking his spaniel with his right hand. A bust of Alexa Harrowby Quince may be observed on the secretaire." That was how they would appear in a Christie's catalogue a hundred years hence. Alexa could not repress a slight preference for more bohemian and unflattering portraits.

John, in distress after Anne's defection, sought refuge with his former teacher at Oxford. What happy chance had made Dr. D. bring him to tea with Uncle Jim one winter evening?

Alexa would never forget her first sight of that tall, taciturn young man, picking his way among the thousand useless knick-knacks which had once belonged to Aunt Sophia, and which, sacrosanct since her death, still put up a fight against the almost exclusively male visitors to Uncle Jim's drawing room.

She knew who he was. And the thought of seeing in the flesh the master of Otterways, at once palace and fortress, did not leave her unmoved. Had she not seen him fleeing the crowd of tourists of which she was one?

Now it seemed to her that she was going to step over the rope which separated the furniture from the outsiders, and that they would laugh about it together. But John was not in the mood for laughing.

He had come to ask old Professor Harrowby Quince a few strictly archaeological questions, to eat a few muffins and then go home. As for trying to please the Professor's niece, out of the question. Still, he could not avoid standing up and offering her a chair, though he rose so abruptly that he nearly knocked over the table on which the cakes were laid out. He sat down again muttering furious apologies. Alexa wanted to laugh.

"There ought to be a rope here to separate the objets d'art from the visitors, as there is at Otterways," she said, without looking at him. "My aunt would have seen nothing strange in the suggestion. She regarded the bric-a-brac that clutters this room as at least as interesting as the catalogued rarities at Otterways."

"Not everyone can be interested in our antiquated affairs," answered John, slightly mollified.

"Even when what you call antiquated affairs represent an important chapter in the history of England?"

John was not, properly speaking, a snob, and the fact that he was the last representative of one of his country's most illustrious families was a satisfaction that had lost its savour since he had lost his loved one. He was weary of the vastness of his house, of its pictures and tapestries, of the whole thing.

"I've taken a dislike to Otterways," he confided in a fit of candour. "I don't know what to do with myself."

Alexa, though inexperienced, was not lacking in intelligence or intuition. "Disappointed in love," she said to herself. She looked more closely at this face, with its heavy, dark eyelids, its full, prominent lips, and took pleasure in tracing a resemblance to the Moros, Van Dycks and Gainsboroughs which had handed it down from century to century.

"Why don't you travel?" she asked, hoping his answer would be significant enough for her to pursue her investigations.

"Why don't I travel? Because I can't bear travelling alone, and because all the countries I like are taboo."

Alexa decided she would have no difficulty in getting a confession out of him. Young Anglo-Saxons confessed so easily!

"You must have something to do that interests you? Even if it's only managing your estates?"

"I have a steward for that."

"Give him the sack!"

This reply on the part of a stranger disconcerted him. She certainly did not lack nerve, this tall, rather faded young woman. He looked at her with some curiosity. Since Anne had gone, women and men were all the same to him. True, there was nothing particularly feminine about this young lady. She was angular as well as tall. She had straight, unenterprising hair, regular features and a noble brow—the same brow as the Professor and as all the scholars in her family. She was of no particular age; at eighteen she would probably have looked not very well preserved; at forty-five she would probably look ten years younger; she was one of those women who, having no bloom to lose, improve with age. She gave a general impression of dignity and poise. She's certainly a virgin, John concluded, and it probably hasn't worried her. Her clear eyes bespoke both humour and shyness: despite her impulsive words just now, she probably blushed if anyone paid her a compliment. Poor girl, thought John, that can't happen to her often. Then he remembered having heard about her books; for the name of Alexa Harrowby Quince was already of some consequence in the world of literature and John was not an illiterate. He had done rather brilliantly at Oxford; his family intended him for the diplomatic service; but the sudden death of his father pledged him to the no less public career of head of the family.

What she writes must be rather clever, he thought. And he vowed to go and buy her latest book the following day.

"As a matter of fact, your idea is quite a good one," he said. "I admit it's important for me to have something to do."

"It's important for everyone," she murmured.

"And what about you?" he asked, fixing on her his ponderous gaze. "Are you working at the moment?"

"Yes, I'm just finishing a novel."

"What's it called?"

"*Yes and No*."

"You like these airy titles?"

"Yes. I like everything airy."

"Then you must come and see me at Otterways. You'll have all the draughts you want." For the first time he laughed outright, displaying teeth that were almost too attractive for a man.

He must have Latin blood, thought Alexa. The English don't have teeth as small and white as that. Go and see him at Otterways! Be on the other side of the rope! Pity the poor tourists of whom so recently she was one! And, since she did not immediately reply, John, used to a more eager response, pressed her:

"Doesn't it appeal to you? I'll show you everything myself."

"Yes indeed, it does appeal to me. I'm just gloating over my promotion."

"Promotion?"

"Yes! The last time, or, rather, the only time I visited Otterways, I was with a dozen other people. And we were shown a door on which it said: 'The Earl's private apartment.'"

John gave another of his dazzling laughs.

"The next time, you can thumb your nose at them."

"Yes! I've always wished I were the urchin type."

"It's a difficult type to keep up in the home of my ancestors," said John, relaxed and at ease in the company of a serious person so ready to make fun of herself. He said to himself that this was exactly the companion he needed—humane and sympathetic and at the same time rather sexless. He could not have endured a very womanly woman then.

The two professors had gone into the next room, where their conversation was made even more indistinct by the pipes they had both lit.

John and Alexa, by common accord, went closer to the

fire, a peevish little coal fire without mystery of any kind, which looked like a papier-mâché fire from a doll's house. Unwittingly they both made the same comparison, contrasting this ascetic grate with the deep hearth in the apartments at Otterways, with their carved andirons and sweet-smelling logs purring like a Persian cat.

Even the fire is different there, thought Alexa. And she felt a sudden contempt for this shabby interior, typical of the bachelor and spinster who lived in it, with books its only treasure.

John held his hand out towards the flames, and this ritual gesture created an atmosphere of intimacy. Alexa knew that long, pale and yet virile hand; she had already seen it in a dream, and now noted without surprise on the little finger a golden signet ring with a coat of arms.

"You have very strange hands," she said aloud. "Almost like a woman's."

"Rather hairy for a woman's hand," he said, flexing his fingers.

"The hand of a prelate by Van Dyck, if you prefer."

"How romantic you are!"

"Like all old maids."

She's always disparaging herself, he thought. Then: "When will you come to Otterways? It's only an hour away from Oxford, you know."

It would be amusing to see her reactions. Otterways would be almost an object lesson in lechery for someone like her.

"Whenever you like."

"You'll have to hurry: my mother's leaving next week, and they're already beginning to put the dust sheets on the furniture."

He rose, and she followed suit. They were almost the same height. John took leave with a vigorous handshake, the kind one gives to a friend whom one would be glad to see again.

He went and said good-bye to his host, and the front door was heard closing behind him.

The massive figure of Uncle Jim, smoking his pipe, appeared in the doorway. In Aunt Sophia's day the pipe never crossed the threshold of the drawing room, and Uncle Jim would no more meddle with custom than he would with the trinkets in the room.

"Quite a pleasant young man," he mumbled, his pipe still between his teeth.

"What do you know about it? He hardly spoke to you."

"That's why I say he was quite pleasant. I like to be left in peace."

"Well, you got your wish this time."

"Oh, there were quite a few archaeological observations before you appeared with your rustling skirts."

"If you kept up with the times, Uncle, you'd know that went out twenty years ago."

She felt like adding that rustling skirts were not the only difference between herself and her aunt.

Uncle Jim, who was not lavish with words, disappeared.

Indeed, a few details apart, Alexa was for him the ideal

woman, silent except when her sense of humour was aroused as it had been just now, and one who could be relied on for silent support. Neither idle remarks nor clichés ever fell from her lips. Not because she had nothing to say: she was the most remarkable woman he had ever met and her learning never ceased to astonish him. Moreover, she was neither restless nor coquettish, and she was marvellously able to do without the compliments so necessary to other women. Poor Sophia—he forbade his thoughts to go any further—poor Sophia was gone, with her canaries and her jingling bracelets. All that remained was her drawing room, in which it was impossible to move without setting some piece of chinoiserie tinkling. Jim used to think, if not to say: "If only Sophia was the only one who spoke!" but she had a talent for causing everything about her to bring forth sounds. There was not one item of furniture, however inoffensive in appearance, that failed to creak in every drawer; not a clock that did not become asthmatic; even her goldfish leaped like carp in their bowl, he used to think in despair.

Then one fine day (how otherwise describe it?) Sophia passed on in the middle of a game of bridge, just like that, in five minutes, and a blessed hush crept over the house. The furniture fell silent, the goldfish glided round in a proper manner. And Alexa came to keep house for her uncle, Alexa with her restful, smoothly parted locks (was it possible for hair, frizzy hair like Sophia's for example, to make a noise?); Alexa with her flat heels and woollen dresses (no swishing taffeta). And the drawing room was the only part of the house to retain the power of speech.

…itherto tuned to the rhythm of a
…m to the slow cadences of a
…p a peaceful appearance,
…et anarchy. Meal-times were
… the truth the meals themselves
…m and his niece would sometimes
…r o'clock so as not to interrupt their
…ght be imperceptibly metamorphosed into
dinner. … then, the meals were never very good, for neither of them was interested in food. A conversation about gastronomy, like those which arise so pleasantly in France after and even before a good dinner, would have struck them as tedious, not to say vulgar. Every so often they gave a magnificent tea-party (shop-bought cakes), like the one already described.

After her uncle had gone, Alexa stood for some time before the fire, doing nothing. She ought to have got on with her work, but she felt no inclination to do so.

The hearth had grown wider and deeper. The shabby little lumps of coal, aware of their unworthiness, had collapsed into fleecy embers, which lent themselves to all sorts of dreams. But between Alexa and the fire there arose a hand, a long pale hand with reddish hair on the backs of the fingers.

"You must be tired. I'll order tea to be served here," said John, after showing her from one end to the other of his vast domain. Alexa was silent, overwhelmed by so many riches.

Otterways wasn't a castle; it was a whole little town, which during the Renaissance had had its own shops, guilds and streets. The butcher, blacksmith and bookbinder each had his own house there.

Shorne had all he needed at home, and rarely went away. The king came to Otterways; why should Shorne go to Windsor? Alexa was disturbed by a way of life to which none of her own ancestors could have aspired. Their highest ambition would have been to figure among the tradesmen.

History had just unrolled its vast carpet, and Alexa stood warily on the edge of it. The past preened itself in all Otterways' innumerable mirrors.

Substances she had always seen treated with respect, and employed in very small quantities, were here in everyday use. You might eat from a golden plate off a silver table—the mere thought was as intoxicating to Alexa as if she'd been waited on by a king's daughter dressed as a maid.

She realized that John's voice, accent and bearing were quite different from those of other men. Was he not the privileged one, the Prince Charming for whom this fairy-tale setting was created?

But that long line of forefathers frightened her: he was surrounded and supported by his ancestors. Seeking a suitable simile, she remembered the decoration shining on the shirt front of the elderly scholar with whom she'd dined the previous evening. The sash from which it was suspended was almost invisible: all that could be seen were two scraps of ribbon, one on either side of his collar. It seemed to Alexa that John was like that decoration, held in place by two discreet scraps of ribbon.

In the circles to which Alexa belonged, people could remember their great-grandfather, but beyond that, memory wavered, hesitated. History didn't show you, with the confidence of a photographer, one ancestor who wrote a sonnet to Queen Elizabeth, and another who died of wounds at the battle of Agincourt.

A subdued silence hung over the little drawing room in which they had taken refuge. The curtains were not yet drawn, and the roughly intertwined branches of the bare trees suggested a brawl, which for some strange reason was inaudible.

It was freezing outside, and the cold and the imminent snow perfected the silence. It was ready, ripe; you expected something prodigious to happen.

Feeling she ought to speak, Alexa ventured at last: "I feel like Parsifal being guided by Gurnemanz, except that it's we who move and not the scenery. Soon you'll show me some mystical scene and ask me if I've understood."

"And you won't have, and I'll call you the *Tor durch Mitleid wissend.*"*

". . . but who asks nothing better than to learn."

"You must be one of those who learn quickly," said John, smiling and showing his dazzling white teeth.

---

* Translator's note: The "fool enlightened through compassion," in Wagner's *Parsifal.*

Alexa added the question she had been dying to ask since they first met.

"Haven't you some Spanish or Italian blood?"

"Italian. My mother's from Naples. We still have a dilapidated old palace there. I'm very proud of my Neapolitan blood."

"What a bore it is," sighed Alexa, "that I can't lay claim to any misalliances! My family consists of nothing but respectable middle-class citizens, much too learned and rather sexless. Our only flirtations have been with theses, and all we've ever carried away is an audience."

John was clearly amused. Her jest at his family's expense was rewarded with a boyish laugh. It was obvious he enjoyed her company. She was so different from all the other women he'd met so far—so restful after the scheming, sprightly, fashionable females who surrounded his mother. She was exactly what his heart, surfeited with emotions, was crying out for.

Everything was going along splendidly when suddenly the door opened and a lady entered—a stout lady of about fifty, whose plump face bore the trace of beauty now in decline. Among features fast disappearing amid the engulfing flesh, an admirable mouth stood out, finely etched and cruel.

Alexa recognised this mouth as a finer version of John's. Meanwhile John himself had sprung to his feet, as if caught out in some fault.

"May I introduce Miss Alexa Harrowby Quince—my mother."

"The Professor's daughter, I presume? I used to know your father very well, Miss Quince. He once took an interest in our ancient pile. Such a distinguished man! I always used to say to him: 'You're welcome to come to Otterways whenever you wish, Professor. You don't need a guide—you know the place better than I do!' What a pretty amber necklace, Miss Quince! I have a collection of amber. John will tell you I'd kill my own mother and father for a fine piece of amber, and he may be right! I hope you'll often come and see us. John's a real boor, just like his poor dear father—so good and kind, but unsociable as only Anglo-Saxons can be. It surprises you to hear me say that, but I'm a Neapolitan and we love conversation in Naples. And then I was brought up in France, so you see . . ." And she held up two chubby little white hands.

"John, I hope you've shown Miss Quince everything—the tapestries, the porcelain, the miniatures . . . everything? Now I'm afraid I must be off. I'm organizing a fête for the orphans in Harrowbridge—our village, you know—very charming, very worthy, but it takes up all my time. However, someone must make the sacrifice, mustn't they? Good-bye, dear Miss Quince! We'll meet again soon, I hope."

And the corpulent creature skipped with an astonishingly light and silent step over to the door, where she blew a kiss and disappeared.

John and Alexa looked at each other. Alexa felt she was undergoing a silent interrogation.

"What an amazing person!" she began. "And how . . ."

From John's apprehensive expression, she realized someone was listening at the door.

". . . how beautiful!"

She could not help a hint of irony.

Lady Shorne's hopes were fulfilled. Alexa often went back to Otterways, and her hostess's affability only increased. She had a curious way of popping up when least expected, for example when Alexa had brought some of her work with her and was reading it out to John as he lay stretched out on the sofa. Alexa had a strange feeling that Lady Shorne was disappointed to find them in such blameless attitudes, and that she was trying to incite John to be less impersonal towards his new friend. But why? It was not natural for the mother of one of the most brilliant matches in England to see her son closeted with an old maid with neither name nor dowry, when all the prettiest débutantes in the United Kingdom were angling for him.

After rejecting various other hypotheses, Alexa thought she had found the explanation. John's mother was behaving as she did out of affection and pity. She knew her son had had an unhappy love affair and been shamefully let down by an irresponsible female: it was only natural that she should welcome any woman who could take his mind off his woes, and no less natural that she should wish for a less platonic association to complete the cure.

Alexa told herself she was just the woman for the job, since the possibility of marriage would never enter John's head. Even if he should eventually fall in love with her, he was too concerned with the perpetuation of his line and the lustre of his name to think even for a moment of making her his wife. The nine years' difference in their ages would come in very useful: John would be cured, and disposed towards marriage; as for Alexa, she would have an unhoped-for memory to treasure. Such must be Lady Shorne's calculations, and her arguments were reasonable enough.

Why then, since she understood what was going on, was Alexa so uncomfortable in her presence? Why did the consideration Lady Shorne lavished on her fill her with such distrust?

Lady Shorne appeared to be really fond of her. She had her to tea in her own boudoir, paid her compliments, and delicately encouraged Alexa to confide in her.

"One can always do with the advice of an older woman, and to me you're only a child."

But the more Lady Shorne insisted, the more Alexa drew back. No doubt about it, there was something not quite right about this great lady.

Sitting with her back to the light under the inquisitorial eye of Lady Shorne, who only interrupted her questioning to pat her victim on the cheek, Alexa could not help feeling guilty. Lots of people would have been flattered to be entertained so intimately by someone of such importance.

I'm too clear-sighted, that's all, concluded Alexa, once more putting her discomfiture down to her own intelligence.

Having fallen in love with John at first sight, she dreaded

these private conversations with his mother. The tiny room, cluttered with carefully illuminated pieces of amber, each one lit up from within by its own mocking flame; her hostess, sitting motionless like a big spider in the middle of her web—all combined to make Alexa ill at ease. Wasn't the object of such an array of strange things to create a diversion, to stun the victim and sap her presence of mind?

John, while appearing to be very fond of his mother, was also evidently afraid of her. Alexa wondered if he'd been chastised a lot when he was a little boy. . . .

One day his mother had asked him to do an errand for her in London. John had come home late, got involved in long explanations, and finally admitted he'd forgotten to do what he'd been asked.

"Come over here," said his mother, in velvety tones.

Alexa could not help noticing how pale John looked.

When he reached his mother's side, she stretched out her plump little hand and gave his hair a sharp tug.

"Naughty boy!" she scolded.

John's features were suddenly convulsed. Alexa thought he looked rather ridiculous. After all, that half-jesting, half-irritated gesture didn't warrant such emotion. She remarked upon it later.

"Mother was annoyed," was all he answered.

"*That* annoyed?"

"You don't know her. And I can't bear anyone pulling my hair."

"Spoilt baby!"

"Do you think so?"

His bitter expression made him look ten years older.

After less than three months Alexa realised she had become indispensable to him. They were on the most intimate terms. There was only one subject they avoided, by common consent though for different reasons: and that was Lady Shorne. On the other hand, they often talked about Anne Lindell. Alexa knew Anne had had her own room at Otterways, and she had glimpsed a photograph at the back of a drawer.

"I mustn't leave it lying about," muttered John.

"Why?"

"Because . . ."

And three days later he found it torn to shreds. Alexa had never seen him so upset.

"It's monstrous, monstrous!" he cried, his eyes full of tears. "To think she dared!"

"She? Who?"

"Why, Mother, of course!"

Alexa thought that was going rather far.

Two incidents which occurred quite close together increased Alexa's uneasiness in the presence of John's mother.

One day as she was waiting for him in his study, Lady Shorne's maid entered the room, instead of the butler, as might have been expected.

"Her ladyship desires Miss Quince to be good enough to go up to her boudoir."

Alexa gave a start, as if an icy hand had descended on her shoulder.

She found this maid, a very curt and correct sort of person, profoundly unsympathetic. Was it because her dyed red hair and extreme pallor made her look like an imitation Queen Elizabeth—an unnerving resemblance in a lady's maid—or was it because, through her being so close to Lady Shorne, her voice had acquired the same intonations as that of her mistress?

She rose and followed the other reluctantly upstairs.

As she opened the door of the boudoir she could not repress a cry of surprise.

Lady Shorne, clad in a dirty old flannel dressing gown, was covered in jewels from head to foot. The famous Shorne rubies, flashing like fire, jostled four strings of flawless pearls. There were constellations of diamonds everywhere: Lady Shorne had at least ten bracelets on each arm, and on her head, pushed slightly askew by her curlers, she wore her tiara.

Alexa knew all this jewellery was genuine, some of it even of historic importance, but it was being displayed against such a sordid background she found it hard to believe it had not been hired from a theatrical costumier's.

Lady Shorne extended an unctuous hand.

"So pleased to see you, my dear! I'm going to ask you a favour that may surprise you. But I know how kind-hearted you are. . . . I want to make an inventory of my jewellery.

Yes! It's absolutely necessary. You may wonder why I ask you rather than John, or Brisk, but sometimes one has more confidence in a stranger than in one's nearest and dearest. Now don't be cross! Strangers are sometimes more disinterested. I've sent John to London, to make sure we're not disturbed. Sit there, my dear, facing me. I've put everything on at once—to be certain nothing's left out. Everything has to go down on the list, everything—even this little turquoise scarab. Come, now. Here's a pencil."

Alexa was hypnotised. Such will-power emanated from this strange old goddess, it never occurred to her to resist. She took the pencil with a trembling hand.

It was only three in the afternoon but the curtains were already drawn and the chandelier lit. The little room was stiflingly hot. Alexa, bent over her task, felt as if she were sinking into a nightmare. How could she escape? There was no hope of their being interrupted. More attention was paid to Lady Shorne's orders than to John's. Alexa felt as oppressed as if she were shut up with a corpse—and a corpse could not have been more unmoving.

I must look as if I'm sketching her, thought Alexa, but in fact it's a moral portrait I'm drawing—adding up her covetousness, listing her vast secret greeds. . . .

Every so often her model would exclaim, in a shrill voice very different from her ordinary tones:

"Don't forget the diamond arrow. . . . And have you put down the emerald cross?"

How long did this torture last?

Reality was rushing away, disappearing with giant steps,

swift as Fafnir. Wasn't this elderly Freya wearing enough jewels, enough gold, to satisfy the giants?

"This diamond is worth all of twenty thousand pounds," said the living reliquary, lovingly. "It belonged to Maria Leczinska."

Alexa felt as if all her vitality were vanishing, drained out of her by the hungry jewels.

"Write it down, write it down," intoned the old woman. "Four rows of orient pearls with a ruby clasp. Two diamond and sapphire bracel—"

She broke off suddenly, as if choked. The door had opened, and John stood there, petrified.

"I'm so sorry! . . . I didn't know you'd be here. . . ."

"I gave orders I wasn't to be disturbed!" hissed his mother. "I don't at all care for such lack of ceremony, my boy. I think it calls for an apology."

"I do apologise, Mother. But the servants didn't say anything. . . ."

"It's time there were some changes here. The servants take things far too easy. Leave us now. We'll expect you soon in the library."

"Very well, Mother."

And the door closed again.

Alexa was more troubled than ever. She could not disguise from herself the fact that John's relationship with his mother was strange, to say the least. It would have been only natural for him to be angry at being treated like a ten-year-old in the presence of a third person. But, as usual, he had just accepted everything.

There was something insulting about Lady Shorne's ascendancy over him.

"Alexa, you're not listening to what I'm saying. Go on, if you please. You've got the two bracelets? Well, add a sunburst set with brilliants. Good. Now all that's left is the little turquoise scarab. Don't put that down, because I'm going to make you a present of it."

Alexa felt an unbearable embarrassment creeping over her, rather as if a thief had offered to share his loot with her.

"No, really, Lady Shorne," she protested. "I couldn't! I haven't done anything. . . ."

"Now, now—don't make a fuss! You've been useful to me, and that's enough."

She quickly unpinned the little scarab and came and fastened it on Alexa's blouse.

"Blue on white—that brings good luck. Who knows—" the heavy face, as of an ageing but still handsome Poppaea, was rejuvenated by an expression of sprightly malice—"perhaps it will help you find a lover!"

However subtle she may be, a spinster belonging to the English middle classes cannot be transplanted into surroundings such as Otterways without some risk. If Alexa did not keep going into ecstasies, if she refrained from showing John how grateful she was to him for having "raised" her to his level, she nevertheless thought about those things.

We must not forget the unparalleled prestige the

aristocracy enjoy among the middle and working classes in England, even today; nor the eagerness with which those classes seize upon everything the privileged class does, applauding and admiring all their exploits like a child at a circus, pleased in advance with all the acrobats' tricks. If one of the less privileged classes attempted exactly the same things, he would be greeted with laughter and derision. England's main driving force is snobbery.

Finally Alexa's happiness reached its peak. She was invited to spend a weekend at Otterways, where everything conspired to make her despise her hitherto frugal way of life, starting with her breakfast tray, with its pat of butter stamped with the Shorne coat of arms and its dish of crisp brioches (Shorne would have been ashamed to employ an English cook). Alexa discovered that sensual pleasure did not reside, as she had supposed, in just one time-honoured act. It could exist in everything—in the way someone lit a cigarette or peeled an apple. Sensual pleasure is an atmosphere, not an incident; a diffused, continuous state; a lens which is added to your vision at birth and which never leaves you until you die. Alexa gave up the struggle.

Everything would have been perfect without her hostess. Lady Shorne had a talent for giving an unexpected twist to the conversation. Once, when they were talking about a family friend who'd gone down in the world, she said, provocatively:

"He's quite right, of course!"

"How can you say that, Mother? You know very well he's ruined by drugs!"

"At least he's tried everything. If I were a man, there's not a vice or an adventure I wouldn't have had a go at, out of curiosity, just to see. For example, from all I've heard, smoking opium must be a marvellous sensation. . . ."

Lady Shorne's eager expression and air of conviction made her words all the more unseemly. Alexa was shocked. Yet she was used to discussing everything freely and scientifically. Vice, stripped of its veils (and thus also of its charms), shivered and shook and could not stand up to examination. The onlooker wondered how it could even have seemed attractive, and how its variations could ever have aroused anything more than a clinical curiosity. Later, when it ceased to be talked of, it could return to the comfortable anonymity of prudishness, where it could flourish unchecked.

The only thing was, the more natural it appeared to Alexa that she should take part in a Freudian conversation on equal terms with three or four young men in horn-rimmed spectacles, the more indecent it seemed to her that a fifty-year-old matron should indulge in voluptuous speculation. Alexa was reminded of something. Was it in a book or a play? Suddenly she remembered reading about an elderly empress of China who, to preserve her own position, forced her invalid son to smoke ten pipes of opium a day.

How was Lady Shorne's attitude in this to be reconciled with her local reputation for good works? Was there some resemblance between her and Catherine de Medici, at once a chaste woman and a murderer, who used orgies to stun her victims, who guided the killer's hand with her own pious fingers, and who wore out her heavy knees on the floors of chapels?

After all, why should she not be one of those old free-thinkers who have strayed into the twentieth century, where they are forced to go always in disguise, where their field of activity is restricted, and where the bites they inflict are counteracted by the antidote of universal mediocrity?

But Alexa was too much in need of reassurance not to dismiss this hypothesis as merely literary. No, the atmosphere at Otterways was solely responsible for the state of affairs that troubled her. Here even the most conventional people seemed improbable, becoming iridescent, exotic, exaggeratedly like some reprehensible ancestor whose picturesqueness had become respectable with the passage of time. The most inexpressive of hands became full of life, stood out on their own, and finally turned into one of those diabolical "studies" in Leonardo's notebooks.

Alexa knew now what chair to sit in to appear to advantage, and what attitude to adopt when John came to meet her in the library.

The morning after her arrival she was on her way to return to the shelves a valuable book which she had borrowed the previous day. It was nine o'clock. A housemaid, kneeling before the hearth to polish the andirons, scowled at her resentfully, as if the latter had come to check up on her.

The library door was ajar. A sharp March sun filled the great room, with its bright bay-windows. A figure in a dressing gown, who could only be Alexa's hostess, was sitting at the Chippendale desk. Alexa saw her from behind, and her back looked absorbed, concentrated on some exacting task. Scraps of paper were scattered all over the table, apparently fragments of letters, which Lady Shorne was sticking together with the aid of a big brush and a pot of paste.

Alexa, realizing she was intruding, tried to beat a retreat, but it was too late. Lady Shorne turned towards her a countenance distorted with fury.

"What are you doing here? Spying on me?"

"I didn't know you'd be here," stammered poor Alexa.

"Haven't I the right to be in my own library? It seems to me you are very presumptuous, Miss Quince!"

As she spoke she had swiftly covered the scraps of paper with the blotter, but the pot of paste was not so easily hidden, and stood there like proof of her guilt.

Fixing Alexa with her hypnotic gaze, she continued, less truculently:

"I was just taking clippings out of the papers." Then, with a sudden dazzling smile: "I keep a scrapbook of everything that has to do with Otterways or the Shorne family."

Would it work? She looked at Alexa with her head thrown back, like a painter who has just executed a particularly bold brush stroke.

"You must put the blame on my vanity. I don't like to be seen in such a state of undress."

Has she forgotten she was wearing the same dressing gown the day she showed me the jewels? thought Alexa. She was amused by such quick-wittedness and thought it deserved a reward.

"I do understand!" she cried, with such spontaneity

that the other woman's expression immediately relaxed. "I have a scrapbook too, for the articles published about my books. I'll bring it to show you one day."

Lady Shorne rose and took her by the arm.

"Ah, but you're a celebrity! I'm only the Shorne family's steward. . . . I'm very fond of you, you know. And I'm preparing a little surprise for you. . . . You're not cross with your old friend for flaring up just now, are you?"

She could have sat as a model to Boilly for his picture of Cunning, thought Alexa, put on her guard as usual by her hostess's excessive friendliness.

"No, of course you're not! Now, I'll wager poor John's looking for you everywhere, and I mustn't be selfish. By the way, you really mustn't leave today—I absolutely insist you stay until tomorrow. No, no—I shan't take no for an answer!"

That same evening John told Alexa his mother had had to go to London on business and wouldn't be back until the following day.

Was that the surprise?

Alexa suspected a trap, but her joy soon made her forget. It was the first time she and John had been alone at Otterways, and now he could enjoy the illusion of being its owner. Alexa felt like a little girl again when he solemnly asked her to sit opposite him at the other end of the dining table. Nanny was out, and they were playing at being grown-ups. Soon they'd be spanked.

Their candle-lit dinner was thrilling. They sat in a pool

of light surrounded by looming, grimacing shadows which dared not encroach on their magic circle. The old butler impassively filled and re-filled their glasses. They ate and drank immoderately. John's tongue was loosened; like many taciturn people, he became rather boastful when he drank.

"I'll wager Anne misses me now! Fellows like me don't grow on trees! Poor girl, it won't be easy for her to find someone to take my place—she's very difficult to please as a lover. . . ."

There was a gleam of lust in his eye. His damp hair clung to his forehead. On the table lay a silver box gleaming with the patina of centuries, and his fingers strayed over it languorously. Alexa couldn't take her eyes off the box or John's fingers: it was as if that caress really belonged to her. . . .

"I wish you could have seen her. She has a body like a nymph by Jean Goujon, with long legs and a high bosom. . . ."

It was becoming unbearable. Alexa hated the absent Anne, the intruder, with all her heart. What had she, Alexa, to offer, in place of all those confident charms? Exceptional erudition? A distinguished character?

Her acquaintance with John had shown her the speciousness of these advantages. Poor Alexa blushed now at the thought of her lofty bearing, her monastic reserve. To give herself confidence she accepted a liqueur, which made her quite drunk.

John had lit a cigar, and was gazing at her more indulgently than was his usual wont.

Candle-light suits her, he was thinking. It doesn't light her; it illuminates her. She has a Gothic face, like a face in a missal—she looks like St. Catherine of Siena. Her pale hair has a halo of gold.

Then: "You look very Christian this evening," he said, half jesting, half affectionate.

"And you look just like Nero!" she managed to reply.

"So we'll throw you to the lions. Or"—showing his dazzling teeth—"or why not just to Nero himself?"

And Alexa, scarely knowing what she was saying, stammered:

"Why not?"

"Come along then, my little Christian."

He had suddenly decided it would be amusing to possess this incorruptible creature. Not without difficulty, he rose from the table, put his arm around her waist, and crushed her mouth against his own.

At that exact moment Alexa became what she had unconsciously wanted to be all her life—a woman, Woman, all women. John had forgotten her intelligence, her learning, her moral worth. . . .

"Where . . . ?" he breathed.

Alexa had the impression she had heard this question before, that this scene had already happened, that it was part of the famous Otterways repertoire. So her answer was foreordained too.

"In the Charles II Room," her voice said obediently.

"So be it," said John.

He loved anything theatrical, and would if necessary have agreed to dress up as Charles II. They left the dining room, with its aroma of port and cigars. In passing, John caught up the electric lamp which always stood in the doorway and which cut through the dark at right angles, like a scalpel. Arm in arm they went up the slippery staircase that led to the state apartments. Alexa supported him. He was the lord, the ravisher. She was about to become his mistress. They had to go through eight drawing rooms in all—a long way for a couple who had been drinking.

The lamp wavered, rose and fell as if making signals in semaphore.

In the middle of the Gobelins drawing room John stopped short, clinging to his companion's arm.

"Did you hear that? Someone laughed."

"I didn't hear anything."

He had the usual drunkard's obstinacy.

"Someone laughed, I tell you! Listen!"

But Alexa heard only the beating of her heart.

The lamp aimed at a Gainsborough and cut off its head. Alexa was amazed to see the body, icily elegant, remain as it was. A kind of false silence returned, as when you're playing Hide and Seek and the seeker enters.

John gave an uncertain laugh.

"I must have been mistaken. Come on!"

There were still three drawing rooms to go through, all three strewn with obstacles. Once, they ran into one of the ropes which cordoned off the furniture from the tourists. Alexa laughed aloud. This time she had left them standing!

The lamp awakened now a Moro, now a Hogarth, now the lacquer surface of a Chinese cabinet. . . .

Finally they reached the two steps leading into the

Charles II bedchamber. They stumbled over one of them and nearly fell. The lamp probed the darkness. The room seemed as vast as a cathedral. Alexa was rather frightened. Why had she chosen such an enormous room?

The state apartments were lit only by candles. John set his lamp down on the dressing table, and immediately a triangle of light was projected onto the astonished ceiling.

Now they had to light the candelabra. It wasn't easy. Alexa watched John do it, her heart beating fast.

She was sitting in one of the huge armchairs on either side of the fireplace. As the candles were lit, one object after another sprang into view. The silver console-table with the arms of Charles II? Present! The Mortlake tapestry showing Joseph escaping the caresses of Potiphar's wife? Present! Joseph and Mrs. Potiphar had swarthy faces underneath their fair curls; they looked sinister, like victims of the plague wearing wigs.

At last all the candles were lit. They cast an incomplete but precious light. The room was cold and musty, with a smell of camphor from the little bags attached to every piece of upholstery.

John, his task accomplished, fell upon Alexa.

"Lie down on the bed," he commanded, and, fainting with pleasure, she obeyed. John lay down beside her, impatiently brushing aside the little bags of camphor on the bolster.

Soon he was muttering incoherent phrases she could scarcely understand:

"I'm the master here! I'll show her! How dare she . . ."

The birds wake early in March. There was one in particular, a goldfinch, whose sharp, repetitive trill may have pierced through John's half-slumber. Or perhaps the sun was to blame, taking advantage of the undrawn curtains and turning this decadent chamber into a pool of light.

Where was he? Instinctively he tried to take his bearings. His old walnut chest of drawers? His paper-strewn desk? The photographs of his favourite statues? But none of these was anywhere to be seen!

As he started up in confusion he brushed against first an arm and then a leg. There was a woman sleeping beside him—breathing as regularly and rhythmically as a little girl. . . .

John's first reaction was one of consternation.

That well-behaved, matronly lady—here?

Then he remembered the fatal dinner, the zigzag progress through the drawing rooms, his sudden anger against his mother.

He felt guilty, ashamed. What a horrible position to be in! He wanted to run away and hide. Admittedly he was fond of Alexa, but not fond enough to make her his mistress. He was in a grotesque situation. He must have been drinking . . . he must have been drunk! His only idea was to get away before his companion awoke. They could talk things over later on. Carefully, carefully, John pushed back the heavy silver damask coverlet he had pulled over them the night before. He heard the crackle as he did so: a sheet of blue paper was pinned to the coverlet. John recognised his mother's flowing hand: "Don't worry—you won't be disturbed. I'll explain to the servants."

Faced with Alexa's gratitude and Lady Shorne's blessing, John had not the heart to extricate himself from a situation that suited everyone else so well. It wasn't the first time he'd been shocked by his mother's cynicism, and the thought of her bending over him and Alexa as they slept filled him with a repugnance that always manifested itself in an angry silence which she pretended not to notice.

What did her intolerable collusion mean? She had been the most virtuous of wives, yet, far from disapproving of her husband's extramarital adventures she might almost be thought to have encouraged them, leaving him alone with other women and creating an atmosphere propitious to dalliance. When he died she wore the deepest of mourning, even calling forth acid comments with her heavy jet beads and crêpe veil down to the ground. "Lady Shorne's mourning is positively Italian! Of course, she's not really English, is she?"

But John remembered the evening of the funeral. His mother, pleading that she was overcome with grief, had dinner brought to her in her room. John found her sitting before a tray laden with the sort of food that usually accompanies a celebration—champagne, caviare, pâté de foie gras. . . .

It's to celebrate the fact that she's now the regent, he thought with a shudder.

When Lady Shorne married John's father, Otterways was going to rack and ruin. It rained on the parquet floors, and swallows nested in the cornice of the banqueting hall. The late Lord Shorne preferred race-horses to works of art, and only five or six little rooms at Otterways were fit to live in.

The first time Lady Shorne visited the place as a young bride, it took her breath away. She knew immediately that Otterways would be the love of her life, and that like any other kind of adultery it would have to be concealed from her husband. So she moderated her enthusiasm and looked as if she didn't care.

"Of course it's very fine," she admitted, "but it must cost a fortune to maintain! Not that one could say it *has* been maintained . . ." And under her breath she made a fierce and passionate vow to spend her last penny on it if necessary.

With what joy, when the old Earl died, she sold the yacht and the racing stable, eager to adorn the beloved, to replace a ceiling or rebuild a balustrade.

No one witnessed her conversations with the convalescent castle. No one knew how, when the day was over and the workmen had gone home, she would lay her cheek against the panelling, marked like watered silk, and softer to her than any lips.

She would have sold herself rather than sell a single

footstool. Her exclusive and fanatical nature, hungry for a "mission," embraced the cause of Otterways with a fervour which in earlier times would have been directed towards religion and heavenly rewards.

She saw the birth of her son as an immediate pleasure and a distant threat. A pleasure because she could bring him up according to the sacred principles of her antique dealer's heart. A threat because one day he would usurp the power she would never willingly yield. Her abdication would be deadly. As after an enemy occupation the rooms would be left plundered, planted with time bombs.

Meanwhile Otterways, reinforced, restored, cherished, smiled at her from all its turrets and all its windows. While he was still an infant, John learned not to touch glass cases and to be careful with petit-point chairs. His was a lonely but sumptuous childhood, nourished by tales and traditions, with occasional appearances by a beautiful lady dispensing refusals and permissions, the second even more frightening than the first.

John instinctively sided with his father, a mild, contemplative man with a passionate love of animals and a languid love of women. John soon came to be included in the affectionately contemptuous smile Lady Shorne bestowed on her husband.

She loathed the innumerable dogs that infested the house, soiling the carpets and sprawling on the sofas. The only one who found favour in her eyes was a pop-eyed

Pekinese with a feathery tail: he reminded her of the magnificent Chinese porcelain *Kaï len* in the pink drawing room.

This complex woman always sought in the real some resemblance to the artificial. When she heard a nightingale sing, she would say, "It's just like my clockwork bird!" She seldom went out: nature struck her as vulgar and unruly. She liked it only in tapestries or paintings by masters. In contrast to her husband and son, she was interested in the artist rather than the subject. "Look at that wonderful Tiepolo!" she would exclaim of a plagiarizing sky.

John, like every young Englishman in his circle, was sent to Eton, where his bookish childhood found him ill-prepared for the young savages he now had to consort with. He read Plato instead of playing football and managed to get himself looked down on. Every so often the holidays would show him that his voices hadn't lied to him; but it was the passionate devotion of his cousin Anne, two years his junior, which did most to encourage his otherwise wilting self-esteem.

When he was sixteen, cursing the laws which prevented him from taking even a dog with him, he went abroad.

Amid the hubbub of the station restaurant at Calais, where whiffs of sea air alternated with smells from the kitchen, John, his elbows propped on a tablecloth that was clean but damp, realised for the first time that his mother was a foreigner, one of the aliens who must once have been regarded as beyond the pale. How was it he had never noticed it before? She alone was perfectly at ease in this seething crowd, giving orders in impeccable French, laughing and making the old wine-waiter laugh too. He called her "Milady" so fondly it might have been her Christian name.

John had never seen her so animated and relaxed. She kept patting him on the cheek and urging him, as she always did when she was in a good mood, to take sips out of her own glass.

"Taste! Isn't it nice? I don't care what they say, Bordeaux never has a bouquet like this in England!"

John frowned, trying to understand.

"But you do like England best, don't you, Mummy?"

"I like Otterways best—I like Otterways better than anything. But I don't like England. It's too simple-minded and soft."

She said this with such scorn that John was appalled. He realised his mother had just uttered the worst possible insult.

Lady Shorne had many acquaintances in Paris who were apparently delighted to see her. John was often left alone in the apartment in the Faubourg Saint-Honoré, terrified and not daring to go out. He hated the bright Paris streets, the taxis swooping about like wasps, the women who stared at him because he was tall and awkward. In London he passed unnoticed. He wrote desperate letters to his cousin, begging her to go to Otterways to see that his pets were being properly looked after, that they hadn't forgotten to feed his rabbits. He'd have been rudely awakened if he could have seen her reactions. "Really," she said, shrugging her shoulders over these meagre epistles, "John's an awful baby!"

Then, suddenly, his ordeal was over. His mother took him to Italy, and there he at once felt at home. The guileless peasants on his maternal grandfather's estate took him straight to their hearts, calling him "il signor Giovannino" and showing him their children and their oxen. He was living again the country life he had missed so much. One morning he realised he wasn't very different from these people. Even physically. Tanned by the sun and the sea, he'd acquired a kind of careless grace, an unexpressed strength which brought out his latent resemblance to his mother. Could it be that he too wasn't really English?

After that he went to Italy every year. His relationship with his cousin imperceptibly altered. He no longer asked her to take his dogs for a walk; he sometimes even picked up the handkerchief she seemed to leave lying about on purpose. They would allow alarming silences to develop between them, knowing that whoever spoke first would say something irrevocable. One day—it was his nineteenth birthday—he took her hand.

"I love you, you know," he said without surprise, as if he were handling some familiar object. "What about you?"

"I love you too."

"Since when?"

"I always have, I think."

Then the scales fell from his eyes and it was as if he were seeing her for the first time. Had she always had that nose, that mouth? No, surely not? He groped like a blind man trying to find something to hold on to. Then he murmured in wonderment:

"You never told me you were beautiful."

Would Alexa forgive him for having loved Anne so much? He was always having relapses. For him, sleep was a beam lighting up stretches of swamp. As soon as he crossed sleep's threshold he was assailed by dreams, quick to destroy all the day's work of reconstruction, indifferent to any progress he might have made. With unbearable gentleness, Anne would lie down beside him, and he would dream that he smiled and pierced her heart with a fine supple green sword like an iris leaf. As the sword buried itself in her flesh, it sent up on either side of the wound a little spurt of white foam, like that which springs up under the prow of a ship on a calm day.

It was at once horrible and delicious.

He would wake up feeling cheated and drained and realise he was back where he started.

His first trip abroad with Alexa did not improve matters. He found himself in the company of someone who had lost her bearings and who flaunted her own inflexible nationality as if it were a flag. And despite his display of unobtrusive French and correct German, the hotel waiters always answered him in English.

Britannia is not to be trifled with.

He was irritated by Alexa's gastronomic incompetence, which made her as embarrassed when given a menu as if she had been handed a gun. To keep himself in countenance he would inspect the other diners, amusing himself by seeking out specimens familiar to him but new to Alexa. The woman of easy virtue, for example, dressed with sober elegance and sitting with her elderly gentleman, but giving herself away when she spoke to the young and all too handsome waiter. The Roman prince, with his proud but weary classical face, listening with half an ear to the prattle of his American wife. The elderly British spinsters wrestling with plans for journeys that would deter the boldest of men . . .

Just as his mother's smiling ease when travelling soothed him, so Alexa's angular awkwardness exasperated him. She was too old to be naïve.

It can be dangerous to move the person you love once he's over thirty. You forget that he's used to relying on his own environment, that he fits into it like a stone into its setting. A seedy hotel room will only lower him if he's of an unprepossessing appearance already and make him look ridiculous if he is usually impressive. Deprived of what the English call protective colouring, he seems as ill at ease as one of those statues transported into a maid's room in a painting by Chirico.

In every country they visited, Alexa, in quest of works of art, would attend only to what was everlasting. "Le vierge, le vivace et le bel aujourd'hui" did not interest her at all. Her rendezvous was not with the living but with the dead.

John, brought up in one museum, was bored in all the

others. That was not what he wanted from travel. He liked to warm himself through contact with living people, to detect an adventuress by means of the labels slashed all over her luggage, to eavesdrop on political conversations in cafés.

Alexa read Ruskin, John read Morand. Alexa admired the wrists and ankles of the Medici Venus, John admired those of the chambermaid.

They were not cut out to be travelling companions.

Once Alexa was back in her own home the situation improved. John was at tea parties to which the other guests had fought to be invited. He stuck close to her side, but he only represented the aristocracy in that gathering of England's intellectual élite.

The men, unkempt for the most part and deliberately ill-dressed, looked askance at him, despising this product of five centuries of leisure. They could not speak freely in his silent presence but had to slow down and go round another way, as if he were a road under repair. The women were less severe; they secretly admired his tall figure, his deep eyes, his cigarette case made of three different kinds of gold.

One of them, Constance Crake, was more clear-sighted than the rest, having a cosmopolitan lover, and she perceived that this tall, taciturn young man was dangerous for Alexa. Disdainful and self-assured, he was by no means the mere "accessory" people thought him. She often saw Alexa throw him an anguished glance, as if to say, "Aren't all these people ever going home?"

"Alexa's in love with young Shorne, you know," she told her husband, a fashionable journalist.

"Not on your life! She just puts up with him because he's fairly decorative, on the whole. She'd be bored to death with him."

"People seldom enjoy themselves with those they love."

"Thank you! But I don't get the impression that you're bored with me?"

"Exactly!" she said, with a laugh that allayed all suspicion.

But Constance Crake was alone in her opinion.

As month followed month, Alexa gained ground. John was soon caught up in a web of habits which made him think he was rediscovering a happiness he had never really known. His unquiet passion for Anne, his fleeting relationships with other women, had left him with memories that were either all black or all white. Now he discovered that the colour of happiness is neutral.

Years went by. John added the memory of Anne as a spice to the "comfort food" of his liaison with Alexa. Strangely enough, his more recent conquests were less piquant, because they were concrete and easily come by. Anne, distorted by his imagination and cloaked in legend, fascinated him like a mirage.

Alexa was less jealous of the present than of the past, but in fact her jealousy was like a squirrel, leaping from branch to branch. Sometimes it was directed towards the past, sometimes towards the present—like now, about the Manning girl!

But my jealous scenes are so weak, she thought, with

a pout of vexation. Completely vague, without any evidence! They can easily be got round with a grin and a shrug of the shoulders. I ought to have tossed a letter at him, as they do in the theatre, and lit a cigarette while he read it. . . . "I found it on the floor when the room was being turned out."

And he would answer, pale and taken aback: "What are you going to do?"

"Leave you, my dear!" she would say through a cloud of smoke, remaining perfectly serene throughout.

Of course, she would not do anything of the kind, but it was necessary to punish him, to make him worried and anxious. A sudden howl of the wind in the chimney brought her back to reality. At the same moment a door banged upstairs. Alexa shivered. She saw the March wind as a ruffian with his hand on his hip and a pearl in his ear. A Franz Hals, a chaser of girls, with wild billows of smoke issuing from his long pipe. He cuffed the houses and made the weather young again.

How could Alexa fail to remember the early months of her affair with John, who went pale at the sound of the wind?

"Anne loved it so," he explained. "It was the only thing she allowed to interrupt her. Sometimes she'd stop in the middle of a sentence to listen. When the wind blew, it took part in our conversations—she paid more attention to it than she did to me. She used to say, 'When I'm dead we'll always be together. My ashes will be scattered around the world. When I die I'll be able to travel for nothing.'

And the wind makes her more beautiful, too. Her hair's made for struggle—it resists repose."

This phrase was engraved in Alexa's memory. Did her own hair resist repose? By no means! It was only manageable when it was left alone. In a panic, Alexa rushed to her mirror, where she saw that her nose was shiny and her hair listless.

How she wished she were small, plump and attractive! One of those green-eyed redheads on the covers of magazines, whom she pretended to despise. Her romantic streak was always ready to surface; she made praiseworthy efforts to control it.

"You're always tripping over your wings," John chided.

"What about her?" she replied. "Wasn't she romantic too?"

"Yes, but it's all right when you're only twenty-two. A girl of that age is allowed all sorts of fancies."

"But don't forget Anne isn't twenty-two any more!" Alexa protested. "She's twenty-nine now—a grown-up woman."

Perhaps he'd be disappointed if he met her again now? Perhaps she had grown fat or faded? Even then she had a tendency to put on weight, as John in his resentment had not failed to mention. Alexa's memory, hungry for imperfections, fell gratefully on this detail. This dreaded interview might be to her own advantage if Anne was sufficiently changed. If she had really got so fat as to be no longer attractive, Alexa would present her to John in triumph. By now she was more or less convinced that everything would turn out as she wished. A chubby, over-made-up Anne already turned a ravaged face towards John, who would be at first incredulous, then exaggeratedly polite, as to a once-loved woman resented for ceasing to be attractive.

Anne was witty, as John had often told her, but in that respect Alexa had nothing to fear. She could control the conversation as a conductor controls an orchestra. No, as far as the intellect was concerned Alexa was not worried.

John liked the unexpected, and this time he would get more than he bargained for. Already she could hear his Rolls purring outside the front door and his rather hoarse voice asking if Miss Quince were at home. Then, thinking she was alone, he'd come in, and . . .

Above all he had to be taken by surprise.

Anne certainly expected Alexa to be a bluestocking if not a pedant. Well, Alexa would be neither. She would be gay, lively, talkative, perhaps rather frivolous. But what would she talk about? It was so difficult to avoid literary allusions. Gardens? But an Englishwoman who likes flowers doesn't go and live abroad. Clothes? Out of the question—Alexa did not understand a word about fashion. Sport? Alexa had played tennis a little in her youth. . . . The word "sport" put her on the right track. Eureka! She had it. Cars! She'd talk about cars. Had she not just bought herself a Buick? Were not the drawers of her desk full of samples of leather and cloth and paint? That would make her seem young, modern, a woman of the world, cosmopolitan. Perfect! And extremely off-putting for someone expecting to have to converse right away about James Joyce or relativity.

Alexa thereupon went up to her room to get the samples. As soon as the drawing room was empty, it was if she had been acting the part of a paper-weight. The door had been left open, the wind swept in, and everything started to fly about. Curtains, newspapers, notes sitting sedately on the desk; even the canary's feathers stood on end. When, a few minutes later, Alexa returned, the wind hid itself like a naughty child, the papers came to rest, and order was restored.

The shrill carriage clock struck five.

They ought to be here already, thought Alexa, hurrying to take a last look in the glass. She had never looked in the mirror so often. Anyone would think she was expecting a lover.

Scarcely had the thought crossed her mind than the front door-bell rang. She just had time to adopt an attitude, sitting at her desk, surrounded by samples, when the door opened and Jim appeared, red in the face and out of breath.

"Phew! It's blowing great guns! . . . What, have your guests left already?"

"They haven't arrived yet, as you can see," said Alexa, pointing to the tea-table, still intact. "Listen, Uncle. Since Jeremy Curtiss is bringing this woman and I absolutely must see her alone, I want you, after a little while, to take him off and show him your books."

Jim made a face.

"I'd rather have concentrated on the lady. Although she can scarcely be more feminine than he is. . . ."

"That will do! Just look at yourself in the glass! You're

not fit to be seen—go and tidy yourself up, and get rid of that horrible tie!"

"I'm going, I'm going!"

And the docile ogre went up to his room, in which permanent and indescribable chaos reigned. It was like a general's tent on the eve of battle, for the disorder was founded on maps. There were maps everywhere, and they had come to possess their own personalities. The room was congested with continents, filled with the din of countries challenging one another. Wherever there were no maps there were globes, but these at least stayed in the same place, though the largest of them, mounted on a little plinth, had once been apologised to as to a lady by an elderly guest of Jim's who couldn't see too well.

All these maps and globes catered to Jim's one craze: he prided himself on knowing down to the minutest detail the topography of countries where he had never set foot, and derived immense pleasure from checking, and when necessary contradicting, the knowledge of the natives.

Now he sent maps and collars, books and papers all flying. "My kingdom for a brush!" he cried, increasing the confusion.

There were no concessions to vanity in this boyish retreat. Jim could never see more than a quarter of his face at a time in the tiny mirror allotted to him. Alexa always said his hair was never tidy except on one side.

He thought it would be tactful to change his tie and chose one he found both amusing and instructive. North America disappeared, strangled, into the knot, whence South America emerged and spread in triumph. One of his students had given it to him as a joke, thinking he would never wear it. Jim knew better.

"That's just where you were wrong," he muttered, as he finished asphyxiating the United States. By Jove, it wasn't a tie for every Tom, Dick or Harry! And with a last whisk of the brush he went down to the drawing room, his hair smooth on one side and dishevelled on the other. Alexa let out a cry of horror when she saw him.

"Your tie!"

"What's the matter with it?"

"It's a disaster, that's all. And I was counting on you to look like a man of the world."

"My tie represents both hemispheres."

"Kindly go and change it."

Jim threw up his arms.

"This house is becoming impossible. It's the influence of those chocolate éclairs. They're making you quite shameless."

"Please do as I ask."

"All right, all right. But, my goodness, you are a nuisance!" And he turned on his heel, to reappear soon after in the crumpled tie he had just discarded.

"It's squalid but intellectual," said Alexa. "Anyway, it'll do. Now sit down and try to look natural. No, no pipe! A cigarette if you like."

"I shan't look natural with a cigarette!"

"Well, it can't be helped. I'm not having the room reeking with pipe-tobacco. Oh, and don't goggle at me if I talk about the car."

"The what?"

"The Buick."

"But we never talk about it. Is this lady in the motorcar trade?"

"No, but she's interested in cars."

"I thought you didn't know her?"

"I don't. But everyone's interested in cars these days."

"Really? Well, it's possible, I suppose. And what shall we talk about next? You'd better warn me, so that I don't go putting my foot in it."

"I don't know. You'll see."

"You're very nervy today."

"With reason!"

"You want me to ask why. Well, I shan't, just to punish you. Oh, how I hate cigarettes! What if I feel sick?"

"It will create a diversion."

"You're inhuman!"

"Ssh! There's a car drawing up."

There was a ring at the door. Alexa went pale. There was the sound of voices: Jeremy's shrill, rather effeminate, with long-drawn-out vowels, then another which beside his seemed deep, almost masculine. A voice that was soft, full of hidden depths, crepuscular.

My God, thought Alexa, I'd forgotten about her voice!

The door opened. A woman appeared. She was of medium height, wearing a tight-fitting, very simple tailored suit that followed the lines of her graceful but plumpish form.

If she wasn't so well proportioned her head would look too big, Alexa noted with a beating heart.

Her features were irregular; her nose turned up, her mouth was too big and her lips were too thick. The upper lip was arched and protruded slightly over the other. The eyes, shaded by a hat with a turned-down brim, were laughing, but small. Where was the siren John had described?

Anne Lindell wasn't even pretty.

Alexa, relieved, held out her hand, which the other shook with a very un-Continental vigour. Might she be less contaminated than expected by French affectation?

"I'm afraid we've kept you waiting," said the full musical voice. "You must blame Jeremy. I'd been ready for half an hour, hadn't I?" she asked, turning to the young man who accompanied her, and who intended to make a success of this first meeting between the two celebrities. Both were his friends, and he expected to get a great deal of pleasure out of the encounter.

Jeremy Curtiss—dilettante, essayist, connoisseur of pathological "cases," Freud enthusiast of indeterminate sex—played a considerable role in London's intellectual life. He had a gift for bringing together the most varied types of people in his tiny bachelor flat, where you could be sure of meeting a duchess who had come down in the world, a former Gaiety girl who now embodied all the domestic virtues, a genius, and a dress designer who was all the rage. He regarded Alexa as the pearl of his collection, since she was more inaccessible to the public than the rest.

When she came to lunch with him it was an event. It was a subject of conversation for weeks in advance, and the guests were hand-picked, unless Alexa expressed the wish to meet an Edwardian music-hall singer who might unconsciously serve her as a model.

Not only did Jeremy keep in touch with all the elegant

society of London; he also prided himself on being up to the minute with what was happening on the Continent. He went out of his way to refer to Stravinsky by his Christian name and showed intimate snapshots of Jean Cocteau.

He was obliging, intelligent, humorous, affected and touching.

Physically he resembled Queen Victoria at the time of her accession to the throne, with his middle parting and schoolgirl complexion. He was genuinely devoted to his friends, though not above "producing" them so that some of their reflected glory fell on him. He was so good at bringing enemies together that in Paris he was known as "Ciment désarmé," a pun on the French for "reinforced concrete" and on his own power to disarm. He was as proud of the nickname as if it were a decoration.

Anne Lindell was a comparatively recent recruit. Jeremy raved over the short stories, half philosophy and half fantasy, which she seemed to have written quite without effort.

Anne did little to help him in his self-imposed task of providing her with as much publicity as possible. She was detached and not particularly sociable, and Jeremy still had not got over his surprise at her enthusiastic reception of his offer to introduce her to Alexa. Jeremy, who had been an undergraduate at Magdalen, had kept on some rooms at Oxford, which he occasionally visited in search of unpublished geniuses.

Now he was in his element. If Alexa, in one of her rare critical writings, would devote a paragraph to his protégée's stories, Anne's reputation would be made. He was as anxious as a mother introducing her daughter to a family in which she hopes to find a son-in-law. He privately considered Uncle Jim in the way—his presence would add nothing to this sparkling meeting of master minds.

He held him responsible, moreover, for the unpromising way the interview began. Alexa, true to her chosen strategy, confronted Anne with samples of leather for upholstering motorcar seats, every so often appealing to her uncle for his opinion.

That was not at all how literary giants should meet, and Jeremy tried in vain to get the conversation on to more appropriate lines.

Alexa, with a triviality quite new to him, was now comparing French and American gear-boxes. Anne was finding it hard to keep a straight face. What demon of perversity was making Alexa go out of her way to talk such nonsense when questions of fundamental importance had prompted this meeting?

But before long Jeremy began to think the two women were using a secret code known to them alone, and that all their talk of shock absorbers and servo-brakes really concealed exchanges about printings and reprintings.

Alexa was beginning to feel quite at her ease. The obvious bewilderment of the two men contributed greatly to this sensation. Between her and Anne a kind of secret understanding was growing up, a determination not to reveal themselves in the presence of these interlopers. Alexa would not become hostile again until the two women were alone.

When the subject of cars had been squeezed dry, Alexa turned to pre-war fashion, referring to a famous woman for whom she pretended to have a great admiration.

"The last time I saw her," said Alexa, "she was wearing a sable coat that must have been worth at least three hundred pounds."

Anne's sardonic smile did not escape Jeremy. "Why on earth must she keep talking of things she knows nothing about?" he fumed to himself. "A babe in arms knows that a good sable coat costs at least three thousand pounds. And what about Anne? Where were the cutting words with which she usually besprinkled the conversation? And the stories about Paris celebrities which ought to have been enlivening this one?"

He made another effort to save the day, but Anne, switching rapidly to English gardens, went into raptures over Alexa's daffodils and started quoting names and prices.

It was too much.

Jeremy flushed with vexation.

As for Uncle Jim, no one paid any attention to him, and he had calmly lit his pipe. His blue eyes were sunk in abstraction.

Suddenly the truth dawned on Jeremy. Each of the women was trying to make the other think she was what she was not: Alexa wanted to seem sophisticated, Anne wanted to seem provincial. It would have been funny if it were not so exasperating.

"What the—am I doing here?" the usually so correct young man asked himself. "They don't need me—they don't need anyone. I might as well go. I'm only in the way."

As if she had guessed what Jeremy was thinking, Alexa turned to her uncle.

"Why don't you show Jeremy your books? I'm sure he'd be very interested in your first editions."

Jim started, as if he'd just woken up.

"Certainly, certainly. This way, my boy."

The door closed behind them. The two women were left alone. Alexa almost regretted her impulse: she felt as if she had been stripped of her clothes. Her latent hostility flooded back to its usual course. Anne was the first to break the silence.

"May I ask you for a match?"

Alexa held out the box and lit a cigarette for herself with an unpractised hand. Her agitation was reflected in the way she smoked it: short, quick pulls followed by long, slow puffs. John had taught her to smoke. Perhaps he had taught Anne too?

Anne smoked quite serenely, as if it were an automatic ritual. For Alexa this formed part of a whole series of small intimacies, like a certain way of sneezing or of settling down to sleep, which took her right back into the past. It was like a landscape seen from a train, an ordinary, anonymous landscape that was precious and unique because the next curve in the line will sweep it away. Anne would go on smoking cigarettes. For Alexa this was the only one that mattered.

She must be a heavy smoker. Her forefinger was slightly stained with nicotine. Alexa picked out one by one all the details John had described to her: the small, white square-fingered hands—Anne must have bitten her nails as a child—

the curved lashes veiling the grey-green eyes, the absurd, impertinent nose. . . .

Alexa made the surprising discovery that she would have preferred Anne to have been beautiful, wily, irresistible—in short, the "vamp" she had expected. It was intolerable that John's life could have been ruined for five years by this plump woman with mocking little eyes and an evident passion for chocolate éclairs (the only thing Alexa had not got wrong). She felt as if her artistic imagination had been insulted, and naturally blamed John, the source of her delusion. She felt intuitively that he would have given Anne an equally flattering portrait of her, out of conceit and vainglory.

Suddenly, unexpectedly, Anne took off her hat. A mass of thick springy hair, curly as vine tendrils, stood up like a trodden-down bramble.

That's what hair ought to be like, thought Alexa, cursing her own straight locks. Like little snakes. Her hat's like a snuffer, and when she takes it off her hair lights up. . . . Her hair's made for struggle—it resists repose!

She was swept by a wave of bitterness and hatred, and felt her nerves slipping beyond her control. If this woman doesn't say something soon I shall scream, she thought. Trying to pull herself together she said aloud:

"You don't come to England very often, I believe?"

"Why should I? The climate doesn't suit me and my husband hates travelling. My little boy's too young. There's no reason why I should come."

Silence fell once more. Then Anne went on, in a low voice, as if to herself:

"To come here I have to leave everything I love. At this time of year the earth's like a beloved invalid who's out of danger at last. Oh, there'll be more relapses, but every day brings us nearer a cure. . . ."

Suddenly Alexa saw. So Anne had not been acting a part just now. She's quite sincere. She really does love her home, her garden, her books, her child. I've been misled. But not by her. By John.

She was surprised at being no longer surprised. She had seen what Anne was like from the moment she saw her.

"I'm so happy in France," said the languid voice. "If I hate England, it may be because I've always been unhappy here."

(Simple and natural, thought Alexa, and perhaps not very intelligent.)

"And are all your friends French?"

"Almost all. I haven't got many friends. You don't need many when you're happy."

Her answers were candid, almost childlike. Alexa compared herself to Cauchon trying to confound Joan of Arc. "If I'm not right, may God set me right. If I am right, may God keep me so."

So was this the creature who had captivated John, then dropped him when she was done with him? Alexa clung to the raft of her own resentment. She searched Anne's face for signs of her treachery. Did not that oblique, rather Asiatic glance conceal an artful mind? And was not that red mouth, cleft like an over-ripe fruit, the mouth of a loose, pleasure-loving woman? But Alexa could not disguise from herself the fact that it was also the mouth of a sulky child fond of sweets. There was nothing malicious about Anne's mouth.

Alexa suddenly remembered an incident John had told her about. One day he was wandering through the drawing rooms at Otterways with his cousin. It was *before*. John was nervous and laconic, Anne was incoherent and evasive. In the middle of the main drawing room—Alexa had seen it since—there was an alabaster head of Perseus on a pedestal.

All of a sudden Anne went up to it, put her arms around the curly head, and planted a long kiss upon the lips.

"This is you," she declared, then fled, leaving her cousin feeling bewildered and cheated.

Strangely enough, this memory was no longer painful: the sharp instrument had become a work of art.

"I like your books," said the visitor. "Especially one of them—*Close to the Wind*. I take it with me wherever I go. What a marvellous title! I admit I bought it for the title—I'd never heard your name. We read it aloud to one another, my husband and I. That seemed to me the best way to appreciate it. It's a dual-purpose book—you can read it, or you can listen to it as music. On the other hand, I didn't like *Conquest* so much. The character of the woman is wrong psychologically. She's much too complicated—why make her into an intriguer, someone false and treacherous, when really she's only an impulsive little animal?"

It was now Alexa's turn to be taken aback, first because no one else would have dared tell her they had never heard of her and had bought one of her books simply for the title, and secondly because the "psychologically false" character now being dissected so coolly was none other than Anne herself.

"Not at all!" cried Alexa. "The character grew out of the setting and atmosphere."

"How strange!"

And she blew out a cloud of smoke. Try as she might to plumb this face, the eyes were full of veils.

"If I dared," said Anne, "I'd send you my own books. But I don't dare, yet."

"Why? Jeremy tells me they're very good."

"Not yet. I haven't yet done myself justice."

How self-assured she is, thought Alexa, yet her greatest charm is that she is perfectly natural. She tells you just what she thinks. Anyone else would have got tangled up in protestations—"Because the books I've written so far are unworthy of you," and so on. But no, with her it's because she hasn't yet done herself justice!

Alexa's animosity gave way to amusement. Why should she go on bearing Anne a grudge, after all? She no longer appealed to John, and John no longer appealed to her. "And since that's so, you run no risk in letting him see her," a voice whispered to her. But then another voice, the voice of prudence, told her to do nothing of the kind. "She hasn't changed enough. That voice. She could still get him back with the lasso of her voice." She tried to make her talk, to assess the peril.

"What is your house like?"

"My house?" The voice hesitated, hovered, then suddenly swooped. "It's old, very old, an old house by a purling stream full of watercress. There are even a few crayfish, and some trout that are not much bigger. The stream runs along by a huge kitchen garden with cottage flowers along the borders. Balsam and larkspur grow side by side with red currant bushes. It's impossible to say where the kitchen garden ends and the house begins. A low front door nearly decapitates you if you haven't been warned. Then you find yourself in a large room that's all askew—full of ups and downs, plateaux and valleys, without any pattern or prejudice. Louis Treize rubs shoulders with Louis-Philippe. Period furniture jostles against armchairs from Waring's. Except in the middle of summer there's always a fire, a sacred and enduring ember. [How she must look down on my little fire, so flickering and so brief! thought Alexa.] I might as well tell you my house has been suspected of witchcraft, and the accusation is based on observed facts. It takes the corners off people's personalities, softens them, kneads them, re-shapes them. Tycoons become lyrical, austere females become indulgent. It's an underhand attack on moral principles. . . . Do you like food? I have an old local woman whose cooking I'd say was inspired. We spend hours together concocting new dishes. Don't you ever come to France?" Then, intuitively: "Perhaps France frightens you?"

"How right you are!" agreed Alexa, temporarily distracted from her goal. "Paris, especially, terrifies me—so lucid, so cruel! I daren't go about there on foot, let alone by car. The taxis look as if their one ambition is to reduce any fragile conveyance to scrap. Even their horns are shrill and satanic, quite different from the solemn hooters of London. In London they're bumble-bees, in Paris they're wasps."

Anne gave a pleased smile.

"I guessed as much. But I'm sure you love Italy?"

"How could one not love Italy?" cried Alexa, taken by surprise. "People always love the opposite of their own country. A prodigal, Dionysiac country—and how wonderful in the spring!"

"I'm not so fond of the Italian spring." Anne's voice came down like a knife. "I don't like it much because the earth hasn't been so ill. You've never felt the case was desperate. The leaves stay on the trees. There hasn't been that gradual learning to walk and talk. Instead there's a sudden consecration, a gala, an overwhelming display of what's excessive. There's not just one nightingale; there are twenty! The flowers, which no one has encouraged because they don't need encouragement, hustle and bustle to bloom all at the same time. It's a rush, a frenzy. Summer, if you like. But not spring.

"If I like France better it's because of her reticence, her secret and suspicious heart. Italy hurries to greet you like a hotel manager; France stays at home. France *is* a stay-at-home, and she only admits her friends, who know she's the subtlest creature in the world. Don't you think that's more flattering?"

Alexa jibbed at this flood of words. She did not like being taken by storm, and felt that this geographical conversation, for all its psychological significance, had gone on long enough. She counted up her gains. Anne, contrary to her expectations, loved and understood nature (a detail omitted by John). She was at once mysterious and candid, impulsive and rational. She was a disciplined romantic—disciplined probably by France. She was subject to bouts of enthusiasm, though she retained her critical sense. Witness her diatribe against Italy. What Anne had said was true enough, but she was getting more and more unlike Alexa's preconception of her, upon which she had based her plan of campaign. Had John misled her deliberately? Alexa's suspicions were like a band of mercenaries eager to adopt any cause. "If it wasn't you it was your brother."*

Of course the first version of Anne was better qualified for the destructive role she was destined to play in John's life. But, as Alexa hastened to reflect, one did not exclude the other. Anne might perfectly well possess all the virtues Alexa had just discovered in her, and yet have behaved no differently from the way Alexa had previously supposed. Anne might well have been a faultless friend but an execrable lover.

Aloud Alexa went on:

"English people find it hard to show their feelings. That's why they like other people to make all the effort. Italians are not so uncommunicative."

Anne carefully applied some lipstick. Her movements were poised and possessive. Then she put her little bag down on the table, like a hostage. She'd finished her tea a long time ago, but now unexpectedly reached out and helped herself to a piece of bread and butter. There was something so involuntary and indifferent to convention in this that her

---

* Translator's note: La Fontaine, *Fables*, Book I, 10, "The Wolf and the Lamb."

hostess was quite shocked. Alexa was sure this slice of bread and butter tasted much better than all the others to Anne because it was illegitimate and forbidden. She must be like that in love too—preferring caprice to routine.

"Do you like people who tell all straight away?" asked Anne, between mouthfuls.

Alexa's heart began to beat faster. Anne was giving her the opportunity she wanted. With a sardonic smile, Alexa summoned up the humour which best suited her austere features.

"That depends on how much time is available," she answered, gazing steadily at her companion. "If it's only an hour . . . ?" (Tone, look and tempo—all were perfect.)

"I've always admired your sense of humour," answered the other, not at all abashed. "I refer to your books, of course. But if I were to tell you all, you'd be disappointed. I have no history—or, rather, I have no history now, like all those who are happy. If I'd known you five years ago . . ."

"Were you unhappy five years ago, then?" said Alexa innocently.

"Fairly. By the way . . ." She slowly lit a cigarette, blew the smoke out through her nostrils, then, fixing Alexa with a look that could be steady as the barrel of a gun, she said:

"Is John still afraid of his mother?"

"John? John? I don't understand," stammered Alexa. All her fine façade, built up with such skill, had just collapsed.

"Let's stop playing games, shall we? It's unworthy of us. I know all about you. You know all about me. That simplifies the questions we're dying to ask one another!"

But Alexa was still speechless, as if her words had run dry. It was she, not the other, who was the mouse. The other had enjoyed watching her childish gambols, had encouraged her to think she was safe, then, suddenly tiring, had struck her down with one tap of her paw.

"How do you know?" Alexa asked her torturer in an expressionless voice.

"Couldn't be simpler. I saw you with John."

"When? Where? How?"

"I was just leaving Avignon in my car when I saw you both get out of the hotel bus. You were busy with your luggage, and my driver was busy with mine, so I was able to watch you for quite a long while. John said, 'Don't you tire yourself, darling—I'll see to it.' " Anne said the words in such a way that you could tell she still felt the scar. What if he had seen her! Alexa had no illusions about what would have happened: John would have been frantic, shameless; he would have run after the car as it moved off!

Alexa understood now why he had been so tense during their stay in Avignon; why, as they entered the hotel, he had exclaimed, "Good Lord! This scent!" She hadn't attached any importance to it at the time, but all that evening he had been nervous and restless, wandering from one room to another.

"Do you still love him?" asked Alexa timidly, realising at once that her question was superfluous.

"Yes."

"Why didn't you let us know you were there?"

"After what he'd done to me?"

She turned haughtily to Alexa, who did not immediately perceive the meaning of what she had just said. Alexa shrank back as if to take cover, then each word revived separately and struck her as harshly as an electric sign. "After what he'd done to me?" Was that it? The suspicion which had offered to guide her, like a ragamuffin in a strange town, was now triumphantly pointing out her destination. The dreaded panorama stretched out below. It was up to her alone to find out the truth. She felt a sudden pang which nearly made her cry out, "Don't say any more!" But she restrained herself. She had to know everything, even if it dealt her love a mortal blow. Not for a minute did she doubt the truth of what was about to be revealed. That truth was already within her, in embryo. She had the strange impression that the person who was going to destroy her happiness had forgotten her. Anne was speaking with a kind of careful curiosity, like someone probing a wound to see if it is clean.

"Yes," she went on, in that exploratory voice, "you see, after what he'd done to me" (She's talking as if I knew all about it, thought Alexa. I must be careful; it's dangerous to wake a sleepwalker) "I'd made up my mind never to see him again. There's one thing for which a man can't be forgiven. Cowardice. He was scared to death. You should have seen how terrified he was when she found out we were going to be married! The dreadful lying letter he wrote me! He didn't even have the courage to tell me face to face.

Poor boy—looking back five years later I can find it in my heart to pity him. He's so weak! No will-power at all! He lies like a child caught doing something wrong. I should have suspected. A scene I witnessed—quite unintentionally, I assure you!—ought to have given me a clue. One day when I was in my aunt's room John suddenly rushed in, absolutely frantic. 'Mother! My manuscript's gone!' (In those days he used to write historical novels in three volumes.) 'Someone's been rummaging in my desk! And you're the only person who has a key.'

" 'Compose yourself, my boy,' she said. 'Your manuscript's been confiscated because you disobeyed my orders. I'll give it back when you've come to your senses.'

"A quarter of an hour later I found John sobbing in his study. I was rather disgusted (he was eighteen at the time), and asked him for an explanation of the strange scene that had just taken place. He stammered and stuttered, trying to invent excuses. He said his mother had found out he was in debt. I knew very well my aunt was extremely generous towards her son, but I didn't press the matter.

"That evening Maria Shorne's elderly maid, Brisk, came to see me. She was like one of those sixteenth-century portraits, with her steep forehead and thin hair like grass growing on the edge of a precipice. Though she helped my aunt hatch her plots, she sometimes warned the victims, and she had a soft spot for me which found expression in mysterious prophecies prudently disguised as dreams.

" 'It's very strange, Miss Anne,' she said. 'Last night I dreamed you were going to leave here for ever. Go into a sort of exile. I saw her ladyship—though goodness knows she's very fond of you, Miss Anne—chasing you away with a stick.'

" 'Really?' I said vaguely. (If I'd seemed to take her seriously, she might have had twinges of conscience.)

" 'The amazing things that happen in dreams! Imagine, Miss Anne—it was all because of his lordship.'

"I didn't turn a hair.

" 'No!' I exclaimed, smiling.

" 'Yes. Her ladyship had apparently got it into her head that his lordship was falling in love, and had danced all evening with you at Lady Batford's ball. And her ladyship thought that was a bit too much, you see.'

" 'Of course,' I said, 'One doesn't dance the whole evening with one's cousin, even if it isn't one's first cousin.'

" 'Indeed not, Miss Anne. That's the kind of thing that only happens in dreams.'

"Then, having set her mind at rest with this precaution, she went back to help her mistress put the finishing touches to her campaign to separate me from John.

"It was soon after this—partly no doubt to prove to himself that he had the courage to disobey his mother, but partly also because he loved me and his love had to have some outlet—that John asked me to become his mistress.

"It would have been only natural for him to ask me to marry him, but he explained that his mother would be sure to put obstacles in the way, and that she'd have to be brought round gradually.

"There could be no doubt that my aunt, despite all her

blandishments, was hostile to me. Sometimes I could scarcely endure her glistening black gaze crawling over me like a scarab. Why was she so against me? What were her reasons for opposing our marriage? John and I were related—distantly, but still related. Though I was reasonably well off, my fortune wasn't impressive considering what a brilliant match John was. There was nothing wrong with my birth: I was descended from the Reverels on my father's side and belonged to the same stock as John on my mother's. But for some time I put my aunt's animosity down to my lack of fortune rather than to the question of kinship. Then one day John told me he'd once paid some slight attentions to the Duke of Bude's daughter 'just to see.' She was a completely irreproachable young woman who was heiress through her mother to one of the biggest fortunes in America. People talked about it. The Bude girl was never invited to Otterways again. It was now perfectly clear: Lady Shorne didn't want her son to marry *anyone*.

"Once we realized this sinister truth, we decided to get married without telling her. John was in a fever of excitement. This act of defiance obliterated the memory of such scenes as the rifling of his desk. He was going to rebel. He would outface her come what might. But meanwhile we must be careful not to give the game away. So I stopped coming to Otterways so often.

"I went to stay with an elderly aunt in London and it was at her house that we used to meet. We had let her into our secret, and since she was as romantic as most of our fellow countrywomen she was entirely on our side. She always referred to Lady Shorne as 'the ogress,' since John's mother had never managed to inspire in her anything more than the sort of mock fear that once made English soldiers call Napoleon 'Boney.' John got a special license. The wedding date was fixed for the 11th of April. My aunt was rubbing her hands at the thought of playing a trick—and such a trick!—on the ogress.

"My cases were packed, we were to leave the next day for Italy, and we were waiting for John in the little drawing room full of photographs.

"We had to wait longer than we expected. An hour went by, two hours. Finally the bell rang in the hall. I ran down the stairs as fast as I could. John's chauffeur stood there on the doorstep. No sign of John.

"I felt as if I were going to faint and could scarcely read the letter he handed me."

Anne was silent for a moment. Her mobile face had clouded over and become as blank as a stagnant pool. Alexa looked at her with the cold concentration of a policeman studying evidence. To her surprise, she felt rather grateful to her. Thanks to what Anne had told her she was going to be able to confound John and make him suffer for once. She and Anne were now colleagues, both on the same side. She was impatient for her to leave. She must strike while the iron was hot, for otherwise her repugnance would fade and she would find excuses for John. Alexa was too intelligent not to realise that she had been given a local anaesthetic and that she must take advantage of it to get the operation over.

The other, her eyes full of absence, went on with her somnambular story.

"The letter said his mother had had a stroke, the doctor thought it might be fatal, and it would be inhuman to leave her. There could be no question of our getting married for the moment. Etc., etc. In short, all I ought to have foreseen, knowing Lady Shorne's baneful influence over her son.

"I gave the letter to my aunt, without a word. All she said was: 'The coward!' "

There was a brief silence. With a visible effort Anne tore herself away from the scene she had just described. Her richly timbred voice changed, became gentle and neutral.

"I apologise for going back over that old story. It must be as familiar to you as it is to me."

"No, no—please go on," said Alexa anxiously. Anne would cut her account short if she realised Alexa knew nothing about it.

"One detail you probably don't know is that Brisk came to see me that evening. I can still see her, like a spy at bay, glancing behind her as if she was afraid she was being followed.

" 'Miss Anne, Miss Anne, her ladyship would kill me if she knew I was here.'

"The 'dream' camouflage was a thing of the past. Brisk, like Kundry,* was fleeing from an evil influence to bring

---

* Translator's note: an enchantress in Wagner's *Parsifal*.

balm to its victim . . . though that didn't stop her from going back to her mistress afterwards.

" 'Her ladyship nearly went out of her mind when she found out about his lordship's letter.'

" 'What letter?'

" 'The letter his lordship sent to you, miss, to say that everything was arranged.'

" 'But I never got it! I only heard the news on the telephone.'

" 'You never got it, Miss Anne, because it was never posted. His lordship gave it to Hudson, who, as you know, miss, is devoted to him. Hudson put the letter on the mantelpiece for a moment while he went to fetch a stamp, and I stole it. He was desperate at not being able to find it. He looked everywhere, and never dared tell his lordship it hadn't been posted. . . . Oh, miss! I swear that if I'd known what was going to happen I'd have left the letter where it was. I never meant to give it to her ladyship. I only wanted to get rid of it. There'd been so much trouble and upset—I wanted to prevent it starting all over again.'

"Brisk's irresponsibility was so frightful I could hardly believe my cars. Then, when I realised that the author of all my woes was there in front of me, I lost all self-control, seized hold of her and shook her till her teeth rattled. 'Do you mean to say you could do a thing like that? When you'd known John ever since he was born?'

"Brisk offered no resistance. The tears streamed down her cheeks, and I could see her despair was as genuine as my own. I let go of her.

" 'But tell me—tell me! What happened?'

" 'You'll never believe me, miss,' she said between sobs. 'I was just going to burn the letter, when her ladyship rang for me. I put it in my apron pocket, and bless me if while I was doing her ladyship's hair the wretched thing didn't fall out without my noticing.

" 'Suddenly her ladyship peers at the floor through her lorgnette and says in that quiet voice she always uses when she's about to fly into a rage: "What is that?"

" 'My heart stood still. I tried to snatch up the letter, but her ladyship was too quick for me. In spite of her stoutness she's very agile for her age. She calmly broke the seal (his lordship always seals his letters to you, Miss Anne), then held the letter in one hand and her lorgnette in the other. As she read, her face went red, then pale, very pale, pale as wax.

" ' "And why," she said in her honeyed voice, "didn't you give this letter to me?"

" 'God forgive me,' sobbed Brisk, 'I told her ladyship that I'd been going to.'

" ' "You're lying," she said, her voice becoming quieter and quieter. "Yet I thought I told you to bring me any letter his lordship wrote to Miss Anne. You have failed in your duty, you have been disrespectful—you are dismissed!" ' Brisk's voice expired in a wail. 'You don't know what her ladyship's rages are like, miss. Do you remember her ladyship's Pekinese? Chichi? That the gardener was supposed to have shot by mistake? Well, Chichi was never shot. I buried him with my own hands. It was her ladyship who strangled him in one of her mad rages.'

"I was appalled. Brisk was sweating truth from every pore. Besides, I'd had some worrying glimpses of my aunt's rages. But on whom was she wreaking her wrath now? John, without a doubt. My fears for him outweighed all other considerations. I thrust Brisk towards the door, entreating her to let me know what happened, and never to leave him alone with his mother for a second. . . . You know what happened next. The following evening John left with Lady Shorne for the south of France, without so much as a word to me."

Alexa felt as if she were hearing that fateful cliché for the first time. "Without so much as a word." No matter how much she tried to see it from every point of view, its meaning was always clear. John was a coward. Anne was his victim. The roles were the opposite of what she had supposed. It was Anne who had been heroic, not John. John was a coward, a mere puppet into whom both Anne and Alexa had managed to breathe a semblance of life. He was as much the creation of one as of the other.

Poor John, poor marionette, he held on to Anne with one hand and on to Alexa with the other. Alexa gave a bitter laugh which made her companion shudder.

"In short, he owes us everything," she said. "He bears our hallmark. He has no personality of his own."

It was Anne's turn to find excuses for him.

"But you forget his charm, his beauty—he's a terribly attractive person. I've loved him since I was a child, and I know what I'm talking about. I fell in love with John when I was eleven and a half—I swear that's the truth—and for eight years I never stopped thinking about him. You see, I was a very naïve and gullible little girl, and John was like a god to me then—I'd have let myself be cut to pieces for him. But when I was fifteen my worship changed into something else. Being fairly clear-sighted by nature, I saw that I was smitten with my cousin. The eagerness with which I sought his approval betrayed my feelings. If I was a brilliant student, it was in his honour. If I'd read all the Elizabethans by the time I was twelve, and quoted Marvell, Herrick, and Pope in season and out of season, it was because he liked them. If I learned all Rostand's plays by heart and agreed to get myself up in Cyrano's moustache and Flambeau's moustache, it was only in the hope of making him like me. For fifteen years I adored John Shorne, and the day after he let me down I tried to kill myself. . . ."

Alexa had got more than she bargained for. She was crushed by all this evidence of guilt. Her former rival had just provided her with a more than sufficient weapon, a two-edged sword that might wound the one who wielded it as well as her adversary. Alexa now had John at her mercy. Like Samson she was preparing to pull down the temple, knowing full well that she too would be buried in the ruins. Had her love not rested on the illusion of John's superiority, on his masculine conceit and his sublime detachment? Now, how could she ever forget the scenes Anne had described? John in tears because of the monstrous liberties taken by his mother; John angry but servile, not even daring to communicate with the person he had betrayed.

But then, how could she triumph over John without also triumphing over the passion which for five years had kept her in a state of voluntary abasement? Should she say nothing, and simply conceal her new weapon to make use of it should the occasion arise? She felt at once that this would be beyond her. On the contrary, her sparkling new cruelty demanded an instant victim, and she could already imagine the scene that would soon take place.

"What's the use of dwelling on ancient history? All that's dead and buried, fortunately."

Anne's voice roused Alexa from her plans, which had made her forget her visitor.

"But you haven't answered my question. Is John still so afraid of his mother?"

Alexa was taken aback and could only stammer:

"Yes . . . no . . . He never mentions her."

"He never mentioned her to me either. He's a curious boy. Ah, well . . . I'm glad he's got a woman like you in his life. I was too inexperienced."

Alexa glanced at her sharply, suspecting irony.

But no, Anne looked back quite guilelessly. She certainly was not very shrewd. Alexa remembered how she had thought of her as a temptress, a woman skilled in every kind of perfidy and cunning. She was not even pretty. Without her hair and her voice, what would be left? Her femininity—that was what made her different from other women. She was a link in an immemorial chain stretching back into the mists of time. Alexa had a vision of a long line of identical columns linked together like vines. Every generation produced a representative woman, not necessarily more beautiful or more gifted than her sisters, but more womanly.

Anne was such a woman. Her symbolic humanity served her in lieu of genius; she was the mouthpiece of the necessary, the apotheosis of the ordinary. It was for her that shirts danced as they dried on the line; it was she who turned an egg and a saucepan into a still life worthy of Chardin; it was on her bent head that the practical sun sharpened its rays. . . .

When everyone else had gone to bed and she had soothed the last-born's last sob, it was her that the gods came to woo.

A frying pan must seem sublime to the masters of the heavens.

There was no reason now why Alexa should not reveal the liking that had tried to spring up as soon as she set eyes on Alexa. How could she show her gratitude?

"You spoiled him," she said with the condescending brightness she supposed to be typical of an "experienced" woman. Anne must not think John had ever been anything more to her than a passing distraction, an interlude in the busy life of an admired and celebrated writer.

"Besides," she added lightly, "I'd be misleading you if I let you think we are as . . . close . . . as we used to be."

"Really?" said the other indifferently. Then: "My callousness may not ring true to you after all I've said. But I haven't thought about John for so long! It was seeing you that brought him to life again. And it's because the life I live now is so full that I can indulge in such excursions into the past."

The plausibility of this explanation completed Alexa's satisfaction. Anne really did deserve a reward. And Alexa thought she had found the solution.

"Send me your books and I'll write an article about them," she said.

"Would you really? You're very kind."

This moderate way of expressing her gratitude, as of a mark of esteem naturally owed to her talent, made Alexa reconsider her rather hasty judgment on Anne's shrewdness. Such self-assurance could only come from someone really gifted. Anne had the unexpected, imperturbable dignity one sometimes sees in children.

"Yes," said Alexa, who usually met with much more effusive thanks in similar circumstances. "I'll be glad to. You yourself are out of the ordinary, and if your books are like your conversation, I'm sure your fame is well deserved."

She was vexed at having written such an inept book about Anne, based on false information from John. That was another thing he'd have to pay for!

"You may be surprised to hear I like you very much. I'm extremely honoured by the confidence you showed in me just now. I hope we shall meet again."

Anne smiled.

"I hope so too. If you ever come to France we'd be delighted to have you stay."

"I'll certainly remember that."

The audience was over. They had nothing more to say to each other. Alexa returned to the heights of Olympus and to her own hauteur. Order was restored. Appearances had been saved: no one had seen the weapon stealthily conveyed from one to the other. Alexa was anxious to be alone and work out her new plan of campaign, but she felt a kind of regret at parting from this woman who had led her through the whole range of emotions in an hour. Round the world in sixty minutes. Magnificent! She'd have liked to keep Anne with her, to turn her into a sort of seeker and gleaner of sensations, half reporter and half medium. "Sister Anne, do you see any one coming?"

She would be as pleasant to have about the place as a plant or a bird: Alexa would have been glad to put her in a pot or a cage. She tried to think of something else she could do to please Anne, but could not, so she started to compose a flattering dedication for the novel she would send her shortly.

Anne was beginning to put on her gloves.

"I love daffodils," she exclaimed suddenly, then rose and went over to look at them. She breathed in their scent with an air of extraordinary intimacy, bending over as if whispering secrets to them. Alexa had a curious feeling that she went over to them because they were hers, because she had made an appointment to meet them here. Flowers were her natural allies, like trees, fruit and animals—everything that grows, sways in the wind, bites and hides. She was one of them, on their side.

A strange young thing, skilfully disguised by Nature as a woman! Alexa had said to herself, "Where have I seen those eyes before?" and the answer was, "In a fox cub." They both had the same look, gold and suspicious. And her hair? Like frizzy little red ferns. Her mouth was a sulky strawberry, her chin a peach with a peach-like cleft. Without stopping to think, Alexa went and gathered up all the daffodils, every single one, wrapped them in a table napkin and planted them like a baby in Anne's arms.

"You mustn't . . ." protested Anne, laughing.

"Yes, I must! Besides, they already belonged to you. Look how pleased they are!"

The daffodils, relaxed and beaming, happily proclaimed their kinship with Anne.

"No doubt about it, they belonged to you already. To anyone else I'd have said, 'Yes, aren't they pretty? They're from Sutton's—would you like the address?' As you know, Englishwomen exchange the addresses of seedsmen and fortune-tellers, whereas Latin ladies exchange the addresses of manicurists and corset-makers. Take them. If I hadn't given them to you, they'd have followed you home."

"You're so kind," said Anne in that warm voice of hers. "I don't know how to thank you."

"You can thank me by sending me your books."

"I certainly shall. Now, unfortunately, I must say goodbye—I leave by the first train in the morning."

She spoke like someone whose task was completed. What task? That of destroying Alexa's happiness, and replacing it with a sharper, more keenly voluptuous emotion: revenge. And afterwards would Alexa go on loving someone now degraded and diminished, no more to her than one of those charming weaknesses biographers smile over when they come across them in a famous woman's life, a Rosenkavalier briefly privileged to amuse an intellect usually devoted to higher things?

That remained to be seen.

"If you really insist on going," said Alexa almost affectionately, "let's go and interrupt the gentlemen. Don't forget your daffodils."

Together they invaded the little room full of smoke and arguments in which Jim liked to bury himself.

Jeremy relaxed when he saw Alexa's pleased expression. So it had gone well! His protégée would be adopted. With himself as godfather and Alexa as godmother, she would go far.

He rose with alacrity, delighted to escape Jim's dull scientific discussions and exchanged a look with Alexa which meant: Well, I didn't mislead you, did I? My latest discovery's charming, isn't she?

Alexa reassured him with a nod.

"Your friend wants to go. There's no keeping her any longer. We've been saying imperishable things to one another."

Anne wore her usual air of reserve, and afforded him no explanation. Her expression was like an impenetrable jungle concealing a deserter in its depths. H'm, that's not bad, he thought. I'll write it down when I get home—it might come in useful.

They then took leave of one another, promising to meet again. But Alexa had a feeling that she and Anne would never do so. . . . She saw her guests out, and the door slammed behind them in the wind.

Jim made as if to light his pipe.

"May I? Now they've gone?"

"Yes, you may!"

Alexa was tense and preoccupied, like a gambler who has just broken the bank and does not like to count his winnings in public.

"A charming woman, that! You came off better than I did." Jim's pipe was drawing badly, and his voice was almost unintelligible.

"Yes, she is, isn't she? She's got personality. But now leave me, Uncle dear—I have work to do."

"Very well, I'll take advantage of this break in the clouds to go for a walk. See you soon."

The door banged again.

Alexa, returning to the drawing room, was struck by its look of devastation. The vases, bereft of their flowers, looked like the jars in a chemist's shop. All that remained of the little fire was ash. And there was literally ash everywhere. Cigarettes consumed by caterpillars of ash lay in everything that could be taken for an ashtray.

And what about her love? Was that ashes too?

It was too soon to tell. Perhaps it would be reborn, like the phoenix out of its temporary disappearance, a severe love disdaining trivial offerings, the love between equals that she had always dreamed of?

Everything would depend on how John faced up to her attack. How could she prompt him to the answers she dreaded to hear because they might take the edge off her wrath? How many times must the Sphinx have been tempted to answer in its victims' stead?

She suddenly missed the strange woman who had opened

up forbidden horizons to her. Her own lingering youthfulness recognized its model in Anne. The slowly assembled pattern of her life had been scattered, and as when the final curtain at the theatre rises to applause, and the gentleman who has just murdered his wife is seen gallantly kissing her hand, or the two rivals put their arms round one another's waists like school friends, so Alexa found all the characters in her own story in unexpected attitudes. The *femme fatale* was seen to be a respectable lady, the seducer had already removed half his make-up and had cheeks like a cherub's. . . . Ladies and gentlemen, the play we have just had the honour to perform is by Alexa Harrowby Quince.

And after all why not? She remembered a book from her childhood. In *Alice in Wonderland*, when the king, a chess piece the size of a man, is about to fall on Alice, she throws her arms around him and shakes him, and he shrinks and shrinks until he is only a pawn.

Alexa, like Alice, had been the victim of her own imagination, encompassed by little creatures become unnaturally large and grotesque and threatening, but who would really fit into the palm of her hand. Like Alice, she had wanted to be the same size as they were, and so had nibbled at the magic mushroom which could make her grow larger or smaller as required.

The little clock struck seven. John would be here soon. She went to look at her hair in the mirror, and gave a start of surprise at the reflection it sent back. Her face no longer wore the look of vagueness and indecision that had made her seem timorous and unnaturally young. What invisible artist had restored to her features their original serenity, their sibylline nobility, putting a steely gleam in an undecided blue eye, strengthening the outline of a too sinuous mouth?

She suddenly brushed back the tonged curls that spoiled the magnificent line of her brow. For once she would be true to herself, true to her own type, emerging triumphantly from the subterfuges forced on her by the desire to belong to a "school" not her own. All at once she felt the charm of abdication; felt tempted to resume her own life, her simple, honest, hard-working life, shut up with her books and flowers; felt tempted to repudiate for ever the way of life she had adopted so eagerly just in order to approach her idol.

She had denied her code, trampled on her principles. Disguised as a woman of the world she had betrayed her own side. Who loves me follows me! But now the battle was going to continue on another terrain: her own. It would be up to John to adapt himself. It is the first discovery that counts. Now that she had the key part of the jigsaw the other pieces would fall into place in a pattern as merciless as it was involuntary. She realised the present John was an artificial character, a summary of all he had read in books or seen on the stage. It was born out of the spleen he had brought upon himself by his own behaviour. Several paltry affairs had contributed to this creation, forcing him into the role of a libertine, which went very well with his physique, and which with Alexa's help, he had learned to play to perfection. He had revenged himself on Alexa. He had been weak with Anne, but Alexa had made him feel strong, and with her he could pretend to be masculine, brutal. He knew he would have been unmasked at once by a woman of his own age and class, and dismissed by his equals, as if he had fought with a cripple.

The other John, kind, solitary and repressed, lived for his dogs and his fields. Alexa had glimpsed him during the brief lulls afforded him by his changeable moods. The good John was his father's son; the bad John was the son of his mother. Fatally divided, he swung between the two kinds of atavism.

And soon he would be here, in this setting that had now gone over to the enemy and become hostile to him. Alexa looked dubiously to see whether the furniture had moved or turned a different colour. No, everything was backing her up. She could count on it.

She was just throwing the corpses of smoked cigarettes on the fire (why they seemed more suspect than anything else she could not have said) when the doorbell rang.

For the second time that day the elderly Jane stood aside to let the tall figure of the young lord enter.

He was in a good mood. He had been back to Otterways and written a letter of acceptance full of hints to the Manning girl. Then he had walked in the grounds with a pack of dogs at his heels. As always, the dogs, the leafless woods and the brisk air had conjured up the soothing memory of his father and the long, silent walks they had taken together when he was a little boy. The silence was always a blessing after the disturbing loquacity of his mother. Even at that early age he had been sure that all the ills of the world were concealed beneath that flood of wheedling words. He used to stalk along with his eyes on the ground, concentrating on keeping pace with his father.

Now, alas, Lord Shorne was gone, and John reflected with some bitterness on how much his own character might improve if his mother died too. He was sorry now that he had been so hard on Alexa, whom, when all was said and done, he could not do without, and whom he promised himself he would console soon. The Manning girl would be no more than a passing distraction, a pleasant episode in his career as a lady-killer, but that was all. But Alexa . . . He smiled at the thought that he felt an almost conjugal affection for her.

So the door was hardly closed when he tried to draw her to him. But Alexa gently disengaged herself.

"Are you cross? Forgive me, darling—I was horrid just now."

"I forgave you a long time ago."

"Won't you kiss me, then?"

"In a minute," she said. And to herself:

"First round to me. All he inspires in me is indifference, if not actual repugnance."

His mouth, so ready to heal the wounds it caused, suddenly seemed like some public utility, available to everyone.

She was appalled by his blindness. How could he fail to realise that Nemesis had passed this way, that this room would never be the same again, that he was now in the presence of an adversary ready to strike him down if he really asked for it. But John was standing staring at the ransacked tea table.

"What! A tea party? You didn't tell me!"

"Didn't I? I told you I was expecting someone."

"Someone—but not several people. Who were they?"

"Jeremy Curtiss and his guest—a lady passing through Oxford."

"A woman? Really?"

"Yes."

"Pretty?"

"Not exactly. She has charm."

He couldn't resist teasing her.

"My type?"

"You usually like them prettier. She wasn't really so good-looking as Pamela Manning, for example."

John, thinking he was in for another fit of jealousy, tried to mollify her. (It was important that the evening should not be spoiled.)

"Oh, let's not exaggerate! Pamela's young and fresh, but that's all. In ten years' time she'll be quite faded."

"Not this one, though. On the contrary. Her charm will increase with age. At forty she'll be irresistible, and when she's sixty her grandsons will confide in her rather than in their mother."

John gave an admiring whistle.

"My word! What a conquest! And to think I missed it!"

"But you know her. As a matter of fact, you know her very well."

Alexa was gripped by a strange excitement. Poor wretch!

She had him at her mercy. She would let him enjoy his illusion of liberty for a few more minutes.

"Who can it be? You don't know any of my women friends."

"I didn't know this one until today."

"Won't you tell me who it is?"

"No hurry. I'll tell you in due course."

"All right, all right," growled John. "You always like to make a mystery of things. Fortunately I'm not curious."

"Aren't you? Good, let's change the subject. Would you care for a cigarette?"

"No, thanks. I have my own. Listen, Alexa, as I'm leaving on Tuesday I was thinking we might have lunch together in London in that little restaurant where one never runs into anyone."

"Very sorry. I'm not free."

"Not free?"

She was being more unrelenting than he would have thought possible, but he did not mind. This little altercation only made her more desirable.

"Not free the day I'm leaving! Good heavens! You're joking, I presume? I'm leaving on Tuesday for three weeks, and it strikes you as natural to have another engagement for lunch the very same day! But very well—nothing would induce me to trespass on your social life. I'll ask someone else, that's all."

He gave her a furtive glance to make sure the blow had gone home, but Alexa was tidying some papers and appeared not to have heard. He pressed the point.

"Daisy March, for instance."

"Why not? She's charming."

John could not believe his ears. What! The very person who two hours ago had made the most awful jealous scene was now presenting a front of unshakable calm. But he was not taken in. Physical contact would soon get the better of that indifference. He rose and put his hands on her abstracted shoulders.

"Alexa!"

Alexa did not move.

"Alexa, don't be unkind!"

"You've often been unkind to me," she said, without looking up.

"Oh, I see. You want your revenge!" He was obviously relieved. "You want to punish me!"

"Not at all. Just being realistic. I see I was very foolish to take such trifles to heart. That's all."

Her voice was kind and free of bitterness. John began to be frightened.

"But I don't understand! I leave the most affectionate of friends and come back two hours later to find someone who's completely indifferent. Won't you tell me what's happened?"

"Nothing, my poor John, I assure you. I thought things over and came to the conclusion that I was exaggerating about certain matters. That's all. I'm not in the least angry with you. It's ridiculous to get worked up about it like that."

John saw he would have to shift his ground. She would never be able to resist him if he made her feel sorry for him.

"How can you talk like that about our love? If, for some reason I don't know, you've stopped loving me, just tell me so instead of torturing me like this."

He scanned Alexa's face anxiously, but still it gave no clue to her feelings.

"What big words! Why must you take everything so much to heart?"

In his bewilderment, John did not recognize the quotation. There was no longer any doubt—Alexa, the keystone of his whole life, was about to fail him. It was the last thing he would have believed possible. He had a lump in his throat, like a forsaken child. He was speechless and helpless at the thought of so monstrous a betrayal.

Alexa, to her surprise, was not at all touched. On the contrary, she found herself considering the forlorn youth with cool impartiality, rectifying her impression in the same way one would correct a drawing. She noted the rather effeminate pout of the thick lips; the heavy chin which would lend itself to caricature later, if it did not do so already; the black but dull hair growing in a peak on too narrow a brow. Only the magnificent, unfathomable eyes required no alteration.

"Why are you looking at me as if you were seeing me for the first time?"

"Because I am seeing you for the first time."

He collapsed into a chair.

"Alexa, you stagger me! If it's my trip to Rome that's upsetting you, I'll gladly give it up."

Too late, too late. Alexa was not play-acting any more.

Where she had expected obstacles and obstructions she was finding only clear roads and abandoned positions. The enemy had fled: there was no one left. It was too easy! The reaction she had so fervently desired no longer affected her. A new-found lucidity told her that lack of resistance would soon bore her. And supposing she told him the reason for her volte-face? That would remove the semblance of incomprehensible coldness which so bewildered and dazed him. She'd be magnanimous and help her adversary to recover.

"You're on the wrong track, my dear. I'd forgotten all about your trip to Rome. It's not there you should look if you want to find the reason for the metamorphosis you complain of."

"But where then—where?" he moaned, his head buried in his hands.

Alexa felt both gay and cruel, light-hearted and cutting. (Perhaps this was youth?)

"I'll give you a clue. As I told you, I had a former lady friend of yours to tea."

"But who?"

A terrible possibility rose up and confronted him.

"Not . . . ?" He could scarcely breathe. "Not Anne?"

"Yes."

John had turned pale. Then . . . then Alexa knew everything: his cowardice, his lies, his abject attitude towards his mother. It was clear to him what had happened, but at the same time he was struck by the improbability of the encounter.

"How did you come to know her?"

"I didn't know her. Jeremy Curtiss brought her to see me. She's his latest recruit. She was passing through Oxford and said she'd like to meet me."

He made a pitiful effort at bluffing.

"What did she say about me? How did you know it was true?"

Alexa's only answer was to point to the mirror over the fireplace.

"Look at yourself in the glass!"

"Just because I'm pale and drawn?"

"Don't bother to lie—it won't help. There have been too many lies already."

He was shaken by an access of helpless rage.

"Wretched woman! She's really taken her revenge!"

"Not at all. She thought I knew what had happened, and I'd have been less ready to believe her if she'd spoken of her own troubles as common knowledge."

"How little you know her! She's cunning personified! She came here solely to take her revenge. When she saw she was succeeding—" he paused and lit a cigarette with a trembling hand—"she must have been mad with joy!"

For the space of a second Alexa was visited by a doubt. What if Anne had invented that more than ingenious story in order to put her off John? Then she remembered that Anne's revelations only confirmed all she herself had feared and suspected. For five years she had carried the secret within her in embryonic form. If only she *could* doubt Anne and her scathing truthfulness! Only doubt could enable her to piece together the debris of her love. At all costs that doubt must be revived and prevented from evaporating completely. Thanks to it, whether true or false, she might recover some of her esteem for John. She had needed to believe Anne for the sake of her peace of mind; she needed to believe John for the sake of her love; she would believe neither one nor the other completely. Somewhere midway between the two contradictory versions she might be able to save her love from disaster. It was sobered, weakened, but she could already perceive its convalescence. Seeing John about to speak, she put her hand gently over his mouth.

"No—don't say anything! I don't want to know. It's better like that, believe me. I want you to answer one, just one, question, truthfully. Were you or weren't you afraid of angering your mother by marrying Anne?"

"Yes, but . . ."

"That'll do!"

The draught had been poured. Without actually following the complex motions of his companion's mind, John realised that his fate was in the balance. His cause was being pleaded in a language he did not understand. A word too many or too few might save or destroy him. But he had a strange feeling that his opponent did not want to win. He anxiously scrutinised her impassive countenance. Never mind, he *would* speak, even if it only hastened the verdict.

"Alexa, you know very well we wouldn't be able to avoid talking about it. I admit there's some truth in what she told you about me, but I swear I can cite mitigating circumstances! If Anne hadn't been so impatient I could have got my own way, but she kept pressing me to take no notice of my mother. . . ."

"I'm ready to believe you, but don't you see the time's gone by for talking about Anne? For five years we've lived in her shadow. She was behind our every thought. She dictated our every act. She was all-powerful because she was absent and inaccessible. She had acquired the prestige of a myth. But now I know she exists, that she likes daffodils and chocolate éclairs; that her right incisor is pointed, like the fang of a wolf; that she has pretty hands but ugly nails; in short, that she's like all the rest of us. She eats and drinks and laughs and sometimes catches cold. So you see, everything's back as it should be, and there's no need to talk about it."

"Alexa, I can't understand you. You've become like a stranger. You don't love me any more—that's clear. But you don't seem to have any hard feelings against the woman who's destroyed everything, who's swept through our lives like a scourge. . . ."

"A scourge? Nothing of the kind! A corrective. I loved you too much; you didn't love me enough. I didn't know how to play my cards; she taught me. She taught me more in one hour than I'd learned in all the rest of my life. She's a regulator, a person who's both practical and sensual—practised in sensuality. She's neither an enthusiast nor a bigot. The mirage we used to believe in would horrify her. Not that she despises imagination, but she likes chimeras to be tamed and on a lead. She's lazy and human, and would never climb as high as the gods. They'd have to come down to her. She likes excess only insofar as she can master it. If she was offered immortality she'd refuse it, like Giraudoux's Alcmène, 'so long as vegetables are not immortal too!' Like Alcmene, she prefers to identify herself with her own planet. . . ."

How could Alexa soar about in the clouds like that, while their love was in danger below? John realized with dismay how far she had travelled, how much she had liberated herself in order to have such ideas. And he felt stupid and helpless, like someone on the ground staring up at a pilot's daring aerobatics.

"You scare me, Alexa! I can tell you'll never love me again. . . ."

"Never as much as I did before—that's certain. But you'll love me more than you did before, so the balance will be restored."

"Do you really think so? I doubt it. It's ridiculous," he muttered, his head in his hands. "That woman just called here, and there's nothing left of our past. Not even a flower," he added, noticing the pillaged vases.

"Not even a flower," Alexa echoed. And she thought of the flower whose name must never be mentioned again, because its scent was too powerful. But secretly that scent would always be her own perfume.

Also available from Methuen

PHILIPPE JULLIAN & JOHN PHILLIPS

Violet Trefusis A Biography

A remarkable woman in her own right and a highly gifted writer, Violet Trefusis is especially remembered for her scandalous affair with Vita Sackville-West, first fully disclosed in *Portrait of a Marriage*. After their abortive flight from their husbands in 1920, Vita returned to England and her writing, and Violet became an expatriate, immersing herself in international society and the world of art.

This intriguing biography traces her life from a romantic childhood – when her mother, Alice Keppel, was the mistress of King Edward VII – to her death in Florence in 1972. A supplement of correspondence between Violet and Vita Sackville-West provides further insights to their relationship. The letters from Violet reveal, as nowhere else in her writing, the depth of her feelings for Vita. Those from Vita, written years later, attest that their love for one another never really ended.

ROSE MACAULAY

Keeping Up Appearances

Daphne Simpson, an educated and intelligent young person of cultured antecedents, is a courageous, attractive, gamine woman, radiating vitality to the eyes that observe her. Equipped with life's most generous gifts she is well able to enjoy herself – all excepting the unrelinquishing presence of Daisy. Daisy, the thirty-year-old daughter of Mrs Arthur of East Sheen (a large gregarious lady with fat pink legs who is partial to a nip of gin) is a snobby, yet popular journalist. Born of the same father, but very different mothers, Daphne and Daisy are seldom apart. Add to this strange duo the presence of Marjorie Wynne, the popular author of *Youth at the Prow* and *Summer's Over* and you have the essential characters of *Keeping Up Appearances*, a brilliant comedy of sparkling and delicious mirth and merriment.